The Teardrop Fiddle

By Francis Eugene Wood

Art and Illustrations
by Robert W. McDermott

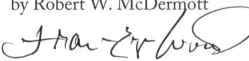

© 2006 by Francis Eugene Wood, Jr.
Art and illustrations © 2006
by Robert W. McDermott

Published by Tip-of-the-Moon Publishing Company
Farmville, Virginia

Printed by Farmville Printing
Photograph of author by Daniel O. Wood
Book design by Jon Marken and the author

First USA Printing

Email address: fewwords@moonstar.com
Website: www.tipofthemoon.com
Or write to: Tip-of-the-Moon Publishing Company
175 Crescent Road, Farmville, Virginia 23901

ISBN: 0-9746372-4-6

Acknowledgements

I wish to thank my aunt, Jeanne Clabough, along with Tina Dean and Jon Marken for their editing skills, advice, and encouragement; my wife, Chris, for her patience and devotion; Floyd and Grace Bailey for their friendship and hospitality; and Bob McDermott for his willingness, talent and dedication to this project. It has truly been an honor to have Bob's work grace my stories over the years. And finally, thanks to the readers whose support has kept the stories coming.

F.E.W.

Dedication

This book is dedicated to my mom and dad, whose guidance and encouragement strengthened the will and imagination of one born to dream.

September 1960

Mindy Fold pressed her feet hard against the floorboard and pushed against the dashboard with her hand as the Ford truck bounced out of a pothole in the dirt road. "Lordy, Barley," she scolded, "have you missed one yet?"

Her husband shook his head and steered the truck close to the roadside. "I can ride the shoulder here for a spell 'til we get to level ground." The morning sun sparkled on foliage wet with dew. A breeze crept through the oaks and mountain laurel as Barley Fold rounded the bend in the road and brought the truck to a stop. He opened the truck door and stepped out.

Mindy didn't join him. "I ain't walkin' down there, Barley."

"Naw, honey, we'll ride," he said as he walked across the road. "I just like to see the place way down there through the trees." Barley peered down at Sassmo's Hollow. He could see the house and some of the outbuildings. It was a little splash of civilization in a place better suited to four-legged and winged creatures.

"We best get down there, Barley," called Mindy.

The man turned and walked back to the truck. He stepped up and pulled himself into his seat, then turned to his wife. "Mindy, I promised 'em we'd take care of the place. I never understood why it was they wanted to live up here, without electricity and all. I grew up like that, and I never wanted to go back."

The woman smiled at her husband. "They was a step out of time, Barley. They wanted a simple life up here away from everybody. You know how everything is pullin' at you all the time. It's what he and Rebecca wanted, and they seemed happy with it."

"You reckon the little girl was happy with it?"

Barley looked ahead as he spoke. "She didn't have nobody up here, Mindy, 'cept for them and a visit from us onc't in awhile."

"I never saw her when she wasn't smilin'." Mindy pictured the little girl in her mind. She could see her long blonde hair and her bright blue eyes. She could see her swaying under the hemlock trees in the back yard as she played her fiddle. "She had them and her music, Barley."

Barley pulled the gear shift into first and eased off the clutch. "Yep, she could play that fiddle, all right. I ain't never heard a young'un play like that."

Ten minutes later Barley pulled his truck into the yard of the house in Sassmo's Hollow. He cut the engine and fixed his eyes on the front door of the wood-frame structure. He remembered his last visit. That was hard. Tears and broken hearts. A handful of people gathered on the knoll behind the house. It was cloudy when the Reverend Gallion said his piece and offered a prayer. Barley felt it was all it should have been, with its promise of God's grace and a reminder that, sometimes, His will is beyond man's understanding.

"Barley, come on." Mindy was out of the truck and standing next to Barley's window. She touched his hand and spoke softly. "They're all in better places now. You know it's true."

Barley forced a little smile and blinked his eyes. "I know it, Mindy," he almost whispered. "But that don't stop me from thinking about it sometimes."

Mindy pressed her lips together. She knew what

her husband meant. And more than a few times she had relived that sad day in her own mind. She even said little prayers when she was hoeing the garden or washing the dishes. Sparkles, she called them. Sparkles of hope and joy she imagined would find those she targeted, and light their hearts in time of need.

"I sent them a sparkle this mornin', Barley." Mindy's voice was soft now.

Barley squeezed his wife's hand and listened.

"I asked for them to find peace in the Lord and happiness in the smile of a child and the music I know is in their hearts." Mindy looked at the house and then back at her husband. "Do you think they'll catch my sparkle, Barley?" she asked.

Barley Fold wasn't sure of a lot of things in the world he knew, but he figured a prayer of such simple beauty could indeed be caught. "There's no doubt about that, honey. It can't miss."

Barley opened the truck door and stepped down. He pulled his wife close to him and took a deep breath. "Now, let's see to tidyin' up the place at bit. I want to get down the mountain a'fore dark."

The foliage in the treetops hinted of an early fall, as sunlight speckled the yard. Dew-laden blades of wild grass sparkled like tiny jewels along the walkway.

Mindy smiled as she walked with her husband along the narrow path to the front door. "Look, Barley," she said as she paused to take it all in. "Look how beautiful it is."

Barley stopped and looked at the yard. Then he looked up and around in the treetops. "There's your sparkles, Mindy," he said with a smile. "With all that's there, somebody's bound to catch one."

Minutes later Barley and Mindy Fold opened the door that Fate had closed.

30 Years Later

Floyd Bailey pushed a nickel into the slot of the parking meter and turned the knob. He heard the coin fall into place and saw the arrow point to thirty minutes. He glanced at his wristwatch - 9:15. It was Saturday morning, and the north end of Farmville's Main Street was coming alive. Green Front shoppers had already begun their treks from store to store. They moved along slowly, attentive to every window display. Pausing, they spoke to each other in faint tones. Heads nodded and fingers pointed to signs up the street. Thousands of eyes would scan the buildings and streets of the place out-of-towners called "quaint" and "time-forgotten." They marveled at its simplicity. They respected its spunk for survival in a time when hometown America is on the wane.

Floyd knew what weekend shoppers thought of Farmville. It was all right with him. He liked seeing the town thrive and found it sad that so many other small towns could not. They couldn't compete with the Wal-marts and the Targets and the shopping malls. But Farmville, the sleepy little college town, had its niche in the heartland of Virginia. It was unique.

The day was bright, and the morning sun caused Floyd's eyes to water. He blinked and reached for his sunglasses. A car horn tooted, and he waved at a local musician he had played a gig with a week ago. He crossed the street and approached a glass door which was covered on the inside with newspaper. He pushed, but the door was locked.

"Hold on, I'm coming," called a voice from inside.

Floyd heard footsteps and then the door opened, and Ben Smalley smiled and extended his hand.

"Well, good morning, Floyd." Ben's voice was deep. It had an appealing resonance to it. Floyd knew the man was a retired English professor and thought a voice like that had served him well in his profession.

"Howdy, Ben," Floyd smiled as he shook Ben's hand and stepped inside.

Ben closed the door.

"I'm so glad you could come by, Floyd." He gestured with his hand for Floyd to take a look around. "Liz and I have been working hard to get this boat to float."

Floyd was amazed at the renovations. The walls were decorated with musical instruments. There were brass wind instruments, acoustic and electric guitars, mandolins, banjos, and fiddles. Pianos, both electric and upright acoustics, were on display at the rear of the store.

"Hi, Floyd." A voice came from down the corridor.

Floyd walked toward a woman who stood halfway up a ladder with a paint brush in her hand. "Good morning, Liz." Floyd's voice was full of amazement "I didn't know you were an artist, too."

The petite woman laughed. "This wall is my largest canvas ever. What do you think?"

Floyd feigned a critical eye as he examined the woman's progress. She had copied the sheet music, note-for-note, and in very large print, for "Somewhere Over the Rainbow." Floyd did not read music, but he appreciated Liz Smalley's ability to duplicate the squiggly notes on a store wall.

"It's great, Liz," he answered. "The whole wall looks like a page from your music book. Will anyone know what the tune is?"

Liz shook her head. "I don't think so, unless a pianist or a violinist gives it a shot while trying out an instrument." She stepped down from the ladder. "Besides, it's turning out pretty good, whether anyone knows it or not."

Floyd nodded and chuckled. "I've never seen notes on a wall that big. It will get their attention, all right."

Liz was an energetic woman, with olive skin, dark eyes, and black hair with silver highlights. Floyd thought she was perhaps ten years younger than her husband. She was thin and athletic and had a pleasant demeanor. Her eyes sparkled with interest.

"Did Ben tell you what we have upstairs?" she asked with a hint of excitement in her voice.

"No. Just that he wanted me to come by and take a look at something." Floyd was curious.

He had known the Smalleys for only a few months. Ben had taught at a university in Georgia, and Liz had given private piano lessons in their home until her husband's retirement in 1989. It was then that the couple sold their home, packed up their belongings and came to Farmville.

The Smalleys obviously loved music. All kinds of music. Ben played guitar and had a passion for folk and bluegrass music. That led him and his wife to gatherings where they came into contact with many of the local musicians. Folks like Earl Carter, Jr., Mac Massie, Floyd Bailey, and others. They became fans of other local musicians as well. Charley Kinzer and the Smith brothers, Gordon and Stan, were favorites of Liz. The couple frequented shows by Trey Eppes. And if False Dmitri played an outside gig for the public, they were there.

A year and a half after Ben and Liz came to Farmville, they began to make their dream of owning a music store a reality. They found a good deal on a vacant building on Main Street and studied the lines of instruments they wished to carry. A retired piano tuner and a self-taught musician with a knack for repairing stringed instruments had agreed to work for commission on an as-needed schedule. The Smalleys could easily afford the investment, and they were too smart to imagine there could ever be much of a profit margin. If the business could take care of itself for a few years, then their dream would be fulfilled. They called their business Smalley's Strings and Things. They would cater to the local musicians and area schools.

Floyd Bailey appreciated the trust Ben and Liz placed in him. He wondered what the couple had discovered that held such mystery.

When he topped the stairs, he was surprised at the size of the area. Its wide floor planks and exposed ceiling beams reminded him of a hay barn. Stacks of cardboard boxes were piled neatly in the center of the room, and there were a few long, narrow tables placed along the side walls. Tall windows allowed light into the room. He looked toward Third Street and saw the silhouette of Ben at the window. The man was busy unwrapping a soft burlap bag as Floyd approached him. Liz looked at her husband's face and smiled. Ben's hands shook.

"Careful," Liz said softly. She watched as her husband unfolded the burlap and revealed its secret.

Floyd's eyes widened, and his mouth opened.

Liz could tell by the expression on his face that he was impressed. But she could not hear the sound in his chest as his heart quickened its beat.

Floyd held out his hands and Ben placed in them an instrument. A violin. Perhaps the most beautiful violin Floyd had ever seen. For a full minute, he did not speak. And during that time, it was as if he were alone with the instrument. He examined it in the sunlight that shone through the dusty window panes. He noted the grain of the wood, the curly-maple back, the perfection of the neck, and the unique seams. He looked closely at the joints. The rim around the face of the violin was inlaid with a white-hickory strip on which delicate teardrops were burned. He thumped the front and back of the violin with his forefinger. He was intrigued with the mother-of-pearl teardrop inlays on the front and sides of the violin's scroll. He felt the teardrops with his fingers and shook his head.

"Well, what do you think, Floyd?" Ben's voice was an excited whisper.

Floyd plucked the strings with his fingers and began tuning the instrument.

While he was doing this, Liz walked over to a cardboard box and returned with a bow and rosin. She handed the bow to Floyd, then watched as he readjusted the bridge and brought the fiddle to his chin. She and Ben leaned against a table and listened as Floyd coaxed the music from the instrument. He stood in a ray of dusty sunlight and played bluegrass and mountain tunes. And, sometimes, he touched notes so beautiful and delicate that Liz closed her eyes, her thoughts drifting.

Floyd was captivated with the violin. It was as if the instrument were exploring his soul, finding and redefining his ability as a musician. It felt right in his hands, as if it were a part of his body. Without realizing it, Floyd played with his eyes closed, and when he finally opened them, the music stopped and he lowered the fiddle and gazed again at its beauty.

"Well?" Ben broke the silence after a few seconds. "I've got two questions for you, Floyd."

Floyd looked over at Ben and took a deep breath. He raised his eyebrows, but did not speak.

Ben asked his first question. "Is that a violin or a fiddle?" His tone was serious.

Floyd walked over and laid the instrument and bow down on a box top. He looked at it and rubbed his chin as he contemplated Ben's question. Then he walked back to the window and looked down onto Third Street. He felt the sun on his face as he spoke. "With an instrument like that, Ben, it really depends on who's playing it."

Ben looked at his wife and smiled. "Now, my second question is, where did you learn to play like that?"

Floyd Bailey was a little confused himself. He had always been musically inclined. Playing stringed instruments had come naturally to him. He learned to play the guitar, mandolin, and fiddle by ear. He had watched others and practiced. He had never thought of himself as a great player. But he was confident enough to keep up with most musicians and even outplay some. And his talent was known throughout the community.

Floyd didn't really know how to explain what had just happened. He felt possessed by the spirit of the instrument. He had played instruments before which had felt good in his hands and inspired him to play better. When he was a young man, he had offered to buy a fiddle he thought was the finest he ever played. The owner, who could not even play, would not sell it. Floyd had never forgotten that instrument, its character or feel. But this was different. This was unexplainable. A mysterious magic he didn't understand.

"This instrument makes me sound better than I am," he heard himself admit. "It's really something."

"I've got more questions, Floyd," Liz spoke up. She walked over and picked up the fiddle and brought it into the sunlight. "What's with the teardrops?" She rubbed her fingers over them and then answered herself. "They are beautiful. And maybe, a little sad."

Ben came over and looked. "They are teardrops," he agreed. "Is that a known mark?"

Floyd studied the pale grayish-blue inlays. He rubbed the small designs burned into the hickory strip. He looked for initials or anything that might tell the history of the instrument. "It's a symbol of some sort. I don't know what it means, and I've never seen it before. I have seen where some mountain fiddle makers carved animals and birds on their scrolls. I've seen mother-of-pearl inlays. But never teardrops."

Floyd held the fiddle up again in the sunlight and turned it at various angles. He looked again into the F holes for a name or initials, but he saw nothing.

"Where did you get this fiddle?" he finally asked.

Liz answered him. "We were vacationing in Gatlinburg, Tennessee, and took a drive along the arts-and-crafts loop. We stopped at an old log cabin which had been renovated and turned into a crafts and antique shop."

"Yes," Ben took over. "They were unloading some old furniture and chests from a flatbed truck. Said it was part of a Virginia estate sale. We just came by at a good time and were able to pick and choose what we wanted."

Liz laughed. "The little woman who runs the shop was taking best offers for practically everything coming off the truck. We came away with some nice buys."

"Anyway," Ben interjected, "we bought an old chest that contained old clothes and some wooden boxes and tins. When we got it home, I emptied it and discovered it had a false bottom. I found the fiddle wrapped in that burlap sack under the planks."

"Was there a note or anything to explain the instrument?" Floyd was intrigued. He had been a Virginia State Policeman and later had served with the Farmville Police Department for over twenty years.

When he retired, he was an investigator. His job had enhanced his inquisitive nature.

"There was a diary in one of the wooden boxes," Liz offered. "I read a little of it, but the handwriting is poor, and it is a bit mundane."

"Could I take a look at that diary, Liz?" Floyd felt the excitement arise in him as if he were working on a case. It was a feeling he hadn't experienced in a long while, and it was good. Since retirement, he had dealt with some personal health issues. Too many doctors. But he still played music with his friends from time to time. And he enjoyed refurbishing old stringed instruments. He and his wife, Grace, had time to go and do as they pleased. And now he had come upon a mystery, a case to solve. It was time to burst the retirement "bubble."

"I'll find it and bring it with me tomorrow," Liz answered. "But, I'm telling you, Floyd, it's hard to read."

Floyd smiled. "Who knows? Maybe it will cast some light on our little mystery."

Ben was wrapping the fiddle in the burlap sack when Floyd looked at his watch. It was 10:30. "I better get to the grocery store," he remarked as he turned and headed toward the stairs.

"I'll bring that diary for you, Floyd," called Liz.

Floyd took a few steps down the stairs then remembered something and stopped. "I'll be away for a few days. But as soon as I return, I'll come by."

Ben smiled and waved his hand. "We'll be here," he called.

When Floyd stepped out onto the sidewalk, he felt energized. He could not shake the effect of the violin he had just played. He felt for the grocery list in his breast pocket. It was good that Grace had made that for him, because although he had read it over, he couldn't remember anything on it. His thoughts revolved around two questions. First, could he solve the mystery of the teardrop fiddle? And, second, could he own it?

The mid-morning sun felt good on the shoulders of the old man as he turned the corner of Third and Main Streets and walked toward the bench which allowed a front-row seat to the activities of the small town he had come to so many years ago. It was practically a ritual for him now to come and sit here on a sunny day during the week. Some of the townspeople knew him by sight and spoke to him with kind voices and warm smiles in their passing. Others were aware of him as they drove along Main Street. But they would never speak to him or even inquire about him. There was little about him that would draw attention. Physically, he was less than six feet tall and somewhat stocky with broad shoulders. He was not particularly handsome. But there was a kindness in his dark eyes and in his smile. An aura of goodness surrounded him.   Occasionally, a passerby would sit with him for a few minutes and speak of the weather, or how the town was growing every day. The old man would nod his head and smile and speak quietly. Children seemed to have an interest in him. But seldom would their mothers allow them to sit with him. Perhaps it was his appearance that garnered the attention of the children. It could have been his hat, which was a felt fedora he wore in the fall, winter, and early spring. He wore a nicely shaped straw hat in the summer. He always wore long-sleeved shirts with the top button secured. Cotton in the summer. Flannel in the winter. He wore vests year round, with a pocket watch and long gold chain. He was fond of corduroy jackets.

Tommy Pairet knew the old gentleman as a trout fisherman who would mosey into his Main Street sporting goods store once in a while to buy fly line or tibits. He would study the various fly lures but seldom bought any as he tied his own. Tommy liked him and spoke to him whenever he saw him.

"Good morning, Mr. Adams," Tommy called as he stepped out from the main entrance of the store.

The old man saw his friend and waved. "Mornin', Mr. Pairet. Nice day."

Tommy stood at the edge of the curb with his hands in his pockets. "You been after those brookies lately?" He shouted over the engine noise of a passing car.

The old man leaned forward on his cane and called back. "Too much rain in the hills last week. I think they'll be hittin' by the weekend."

"It's a shame we didn't get some of that rain."

"Sure is, Mr. Pairet. It's pourin' all around us."

Tommy looked up North Main Street and saw a loaded pulpwood truck coming. He spoke quickly. "Well, come on over when you can. We got some new woolly buggers and elk caddis flies in yesterday. Some nymphs, too." Tommy turned back toward his store.

"I'll be in directly," called the old man as he leaned back. He liked to look at the new lures and the gear and whatnots in Pairet's store. And he liked the attention and courtesy Tommy showed him, although he was not a high-paying customer. It was down home all the way. And that's what he liked about Farmville. There was still plenty of that left.

The old man crossed one leg over the other and raised his face to the sun. The warmth felt good on his eyelids. He watched the pulpwood truck go by and listened to each gear the driver found even after the truck had pulled out of sight. Then he looked down at his side and at the thing he had carried under his arm that morning. Something so precious that fishing lures and shiny whatnots and even perfect days beside streams teeming with trout paled in comparison. He wanted so to touch it. To feel its smoothness and its turns. But he dared not. Not where people could see him. No. The precious thing was not to be unveiled alongside a busy street. He touched the bag it was wrapped in and felt the surge of emotion within himself. It was almost too much for him to comprehend. He knew it would take a lot of time to understand. The word "miracle" came to his mind. But with that word came memories. Perhaps if he were beside a stream in the mountains or even alone in the woods or in his home, he would be able to open the door wide on those memories. But not on the main street of a little town. He would be able to deal with it later. He picked up the thing he cherished and tucked it under his arm. Then he rose and stepped off the sidewalk onto the street. He walked toward Pairet's store and tried to replace his thoughts with sparkling streams and darting brookies.

A week later, Ben Smalley opened the front door of his music store and looked east toward the Main Street intersection. A car rushed past on its way west and sent a spray of water up onto the sidewalk. He breathed in the moist air. The smell of rain was good. He had missed it. He noticed a lone earthworm struggling over the wet sidewalk. He watched it as it found a muddy crevice and slithered into the brown murk. A car horn blew, and he waved at a hand on the foggy side of a windshield. He looked at the sky. The rain had set in. It was a day he would not mind working indoors. Turning, he caught a glimpse of a man rounding the corner of Dove's Shoe Shop. The man's gait was familiar even in its accelerated mode. Ben waited in the doorway as the man approached.

"Well, good morning, Ben." Floyd Bailey stomped his feet and let down his umbrella under the awning of Smalley's Strings and Things Music Shop.

"Floyd, come on in." Ben extended his hand, and

Floyd grasped it firmly as he stepped through the doorway.

"Hello, Floyd." Liz's voice came from the rear of the store where she was busy with paints and brushes and posterboard.

Floyd waved his hand and smiled. He propped the umbrella against the door hinge and looked around. "I'm impressed," he said as he surveyed the progress the Smalleys had made in the time since he was last there. "You could open tomorrow."

Ben chuckled. "We have come along pretty fast with it. And, truth is, Liz and I have been talking about a July opening. We've made some good contacts with local schools, and it seems as if local musicians are excited about a music store opening in town." Ben rubbed his chin and nodded his head as if he were convincing himself of a good idea on the spot. "Yes, the first week in July might be just right."

"That'll work," Floyd agreed. He looked at the acoustic guitars arranged neatly along the wall to his right. There were Martins and Gibsons, Ovations and Alvarezes. Beautiful instruments that would sell to the conservative, right up to the big spenders. He touched a lower priced acoustic with a blond face and simple design. "These Blue Ridge gitboxes are fine instruments for the money. You watch 'em. The bluegrass players are going to go after the company to make 'em better." He tapped the guitar with his knuckle and added, "Nice sounding guitars. You watch what happens with them."

Ben Smalley agreed with his friend. The sound

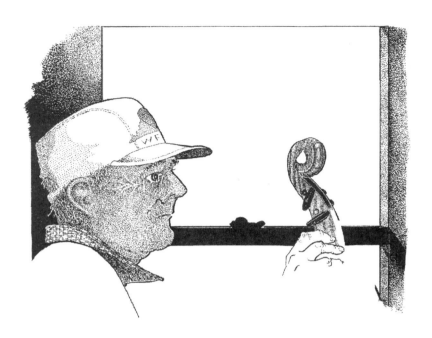

and quality had to be there, or the maker's name would sink into oblivion. "You're right, Floyd. That's a quality instrument with an affordable price tag."

Floyd scanned the walls, glass table tops, and enclosures. "You and Liz have something for everyone, Ben. And you have displayed it so nicely."

Liz had put down her paint brush and now stood next to her husband. Her face was animated when she said, "Floyd, you have got to see something we bought." As she spoke, she reached behind a counter and brought out a small case. Floyd saw instantly that it was a fiddle case.

Liz laid the case on the glass table top and opened it with care. Floyd stepped closer as Liz lifted the instrument and offered it to him. He took the violin and held it at arms length, absorbing its beauty. He could feel its age instantly. Its modeling was superb, and the fine grains of wood had a golden brown finish. He plucked on the strings as Ben offered him a bow. Taking the bow in his hand, Floyd lifted the violin to his desired position and played. He began with a mountain tune and ended with a lullaby. When he finished, he studied the instrument again.

"It's a Roth," Ben spoke up. "German. Handmade. 1920s."

"Where did you get it?" Floyd placed the instrument back in its case and leaned over it.

Liz answered. "An estate sale over in Augusta County a couple of days ago."

Ben smiled and spoke quietly, "I don't think they knew what they had. In the paper they listed it as an EHR fiddle with case."

"This ain't no fiddle, Ben." Floyd plucked the strings as he mused.

"No, it's no fiddle. It's handmade by Ernst Heinrich Roth. My research is that it's worth around $10,000."

Floyd shook his head. "Well, what are you going to do with it?"

"We're going to give it away," Liz said proudly.

Floyd blinked his eyes in amazement and looked at the woman in disbelief. "You're gonna what?"

"Give it away." Liz repeated.

"In a contest," Ben added. "We are going to have a contest in conjunction with our grand opening and give it to the best player."

Floyd was truly impressed. "And who is invited to participate?"

"Anyone who wants to. Young and old. Bluegrass, pop, or classical. We don't care." Liz talked excitedly. "But you get only one chance to become a finalist. Judges' decision is final."

"But how can you afford to give this away?" Floyd asked.

Ben closed the case and answered. "We bought it at a fraction of its cost. They just didn't know what they had. And once the word gets around that we're giving away a Roth violin, well, folks will certainly be talking about it."

"It's going to be a great promotion." Liz patted the closed case.

"I'd say so," Floyd agreed.

"Will you be one of the judges, Floyd?" Liz asked with a smile.

"Oh, I don't know if I'm qualified for that," Floyd protested. "I just mess around with the fiddle."

"But, you know good when you hear it," Ben interjected.

Floyd laughed. "Ben, to win this instrument, someone needs to be better than just good."

"Well, Floyd," Liz said, "you'll know that when you hear it."

Floyd pondered the idea for a minute, then answered. "All right. I'll be a judge. But, if I get run out of town for it, I'll need to take at least one of those Martin guitars with me." The retired policeman smiled.

"It's a deal, then." Ben shook Floyd's hand.

Floyd took a few steps toward the back of the store then stopped and asked about the one thing for which he had come. "The teardrop fiddle—could I play it again?"

Before he even asked the question, he noticed a look from Liz's eyes to her husband. It was a look of questioning, with perhaps a hint of guilt.

Ben cleared his throat and spoke. "Well, Floyd, we really wanted this Roth violin, and practically all of our cash is tied up in the store." He paused as if to allow the words to settle in. "So, when the opportunity to sell the fiddle came at us from out of the blue, um, well, we took it."

"You sold it." Floyd heard himself speak flatly. Inside he was crushed. He felt a little anger with his disappointment. And yet, he knew he shouldn't. He could have told them he was interested. He could have called before he left town that day and asked them to consider him first if they chose to sell the fiddle. But he did not. And now, it was gone. Floyd smiled sadly and hung his head.

"I'm sorry, Floyd. We didn't know you wanted it. If we had known, we'd...." Liz's voice was sincere.

Floyd motioned with his hand that her apology was not needed. "I should have called you before I left. I had that fiddle on my mind since I first saw it," he explained. "You remember when you asked if it was a fiddle or a violin?"

Ben and Liz both nodded their heads.

"Well, I said that was up to the player." He walked

over and touched the case of the instrument he had just played. "This Roth is a violin. The tone is warm and balanced. It lends itself to sophisticated music. Concertos. Orchestras." He paused as if searching for the right words before he continued. "But the teardrop fiddle is somehow that and more. As much as I wish, I would not even come close to bringing the potential out of that instrument. There is a balanced sweetness to its tone. The mellowness is there. And then I could touch a brightness in the instrument that hints of a history born of the mountains."

Silence followed Floyd's words. He had never heard himself describe an instrument so poetically. But then, until a week ago, he had never played the teardrop fiddle.

Floyd did not intend to berate or belittle the Smalley's choice to sell the fiddle. So he spoke to them in a serious tone. "The Roth is a prize for sure. And it will be coveted by all who hear about it. Your contest will pull in a lot of players, and we're going to hear some very talented musicians. That's as it should be. That Roth needs to be in the hands of a true musician."

"And the teardrop fiddle?" Liz looked at Floyd with a raised eyebrow.

"That, too, Liz," he said.

"Well, I don't know if it ended up in the hands of a worthy player or not," Ben admitted.

"Who bought it?" Floyd was curious.

Ben looked over at his wife.

Liz spoke. "A Mr. Adams. I didn't get a first name. He paid cash."

"Did he play the fiddle?" Floyd asked.

"No," replied Liz. "It was the strangest thing." She continued, "I had brought the fiddle downstairs and was looking at it and plucking the strings a little when this old man appeared at the door."

"Yes," added Ben. "I had left the door ajar when I went up the street, and the old man must have heard a few notes as he passed by."

"He didn't come into the store at first," Liz remembered. "Just poked his head in and said he was looking forward to our store's opening. I plucked the strings a few more times, and he asked if he could see the instrument. Said he had heard the notes from out on the sidewalk." Liz paused and Floyd noted a curious look on her face. She continued. "I thought it was a little odd that he had heard the notes, because I didn't pluck the strings very hard at all. Anyway, I told him to come in, and as he approached, a look came over his face that was so sad. For a moment, I didn't know what to say. And then I asked him if he was all right. He smiled without looking at me and nodded his head."

"I came back about that time," Ben offered. "I've seen the old fellow around town but never talked to him. He comes to some of the bluegrass shows around the area. He doesn't talk to anyone in particular, and stays to himself. Seems to be a nice old fellow, though, just quiet. Do you know him, Floyd?"

Floyd Bailey never forgot a face. And names usually stuck with him, too. He did not know the old man by name, but the face he knew.

"I've seen him at a few shows," Floyd responded.

"Usually he's just a face that appears in a crowd for a second. He'll nod and smile at me sometimes when I'm playing. Once he told me he liked my fiddlin' on a tune and showed some interest in the fiddle I had restored and was using. As a matter of fact, he told me a lot about that particular fiddle. He said it was German made by a name I can't remember." Floyd tried to recall the name the old gentleman had told him, but finally shook his head and chuckled. "Anyway, the old man told me not to give it away."

"Did you take his advice?" Ben Smalley knew Floyd refurbished old stringed instruments in his spare time.

Floyd winked. "Oh, yeah. I got my investment back several times over on that one. Wish I had it today."

Liz spoke up. "That nice old man said that if the fiddle was for sale, he'd like to buy it. Ben and I hadn't even really talked about selling it, but then…." She looked at her husband, and he took over the conversation.

"Yes, we just decided on the spot with a quick look at each other that if we could get something for the fiddle, why not? So I told the gentleman to make us an offer." Ben rolled his eyes before he continued. "Well, you know the old cliche you can't judge a book by its cover?"

Floyd nodded. "Yep."

Ben grinned. "It's truer than you know, Floyd. Especially around these parts. I've always heard that you should never underestimate a man's wealth or wisdom by the clothes on his back. In most cases, he's got one or the other, and, sometimes, both."

Floyd smiled. He had come to know this truth many years ago. "What did he do, Ben?"

"He pulled a leather wallet from his ragged coat pocket and laid five one-thousand-dollar bills on the table without saying a word." Ben let his words sink in before he spoke again. "Liz and I just looked at each other and said 'deal!'"

Liz spoke up. "Of course, you can imagine the expense of opening this store, and then we had purchased that Roth the day before. And we didn't pay half of that for the Roth. So, it was a pretty sweet deal."

"I don't blame you at all," Floyd heard himself saying. "His offer was out of my ballpark. But…." He was curious. "You said he didn't even touch the instrument, or ask anything about it?"

"Oh, when I handed it to him, he did ask where we had come upon the instrument," Ben answered. "We told him about the antique store in Tennessee and the false bottom in the trunk."

"I didn't mention the diary I told you about, Floyd," Liz said as she bent down and reached into her bag. When she stood up, she handed Floyd a worn, stuffed book which was bound together with a leather thong.

Floyd took the book and turned it over in his hands. He could smell its age.

"The lady that kept that journal was illiterate," Liz advised. "And it's very difficult to read. I tried and just had to stop. She scratches out her words phonetically.

You'll be amazed at the time span. She writes small, like she wanted to fit a lifetime in those pages. There are little drawings in there, along with daily events in her life, and even poems." Liz reached over and thumped the cover of the book with her finger. "And I'll bet the mystery of the teardrop fiddle is in there somewhere."

Floyd looked at his watch. "I've got to get up the street," he said as he turned. "I'll get the journal back to you as soon as I can," he promised.

Liz waved her hand. "Don't bother, Floyd. It's yours."

Floyd tucked the old journal under his arm and retrieved his umbrella. He bid farewell to the Smalleys and stepped out into the rain. There were errands to run before he would get back home that day. He set his pace, but his mind was on the teardrop fiddle and the old man who bought it.

"Becca." The old man spoke softly so that he would not startle his wife who was sleeping in her chair. The late afternoon sun shone through the window and bathed the woman's smooth face with a golden hue. The man remembered her as a teenager. He could see her youthful beauty even now as she slept. So many years had passed. So much happiness. So much sorrow. Together they had lived a quiet life, away from the bustle and roar of society. It was what he had wanted. It was what she told him she wanted. "The closest faraway place," she had once said when they were young lovers. That was where she wanted to live with him. And so they found a place on the edge of civilization, where birds sang them awake in the mornings and a brook trickled its lullaby through the night. Their bodies moved as the sway of the trees which surrounded them. And nature's small tunes meshed with their spirits. It was a perfect life for the young man and woman. He at his craft. She at her whims. For years they lived a poetic life in harmony with nature until, one day, life became even sweeter.

The old man remembered. "Becca," he repeated in a whisper. Slowly the woman opened her eyes and looked upon the face of her husband. Her lips creased into the smile that had won his heart as a youth. "Hello, old man," she said playfully, sleepily. "I thought you had forgotten about me."

The man covered her hand with his and smiled reassuringly, "If I had only one memory left, you would be in the center of it, Becca."

She felt the warmth of his hand on hers and heard the sincerity in his voice.

"How was your trip into Farmville?" she asked with interest. Becca Adams seldom left the house. It strained her body to walk more than a short distance. Her outings now were usually no further than the front or back porches and, sometimes, a chair under a silver maple in the front yard. She still managed to attend church on most Sundays. Osteoporosis had taken its toll, and she knew that before long she would not be able to leave the house at all. It was a sad reality for a woman who had lived an active life. She missed the walks in the woods with her husband. She missed the sparkling trout streams they frequented, and the warm glow of campfires they had slept beside. The vistas from the mountain peaks of the Blue Ridge were etched in her memory. Mountain peaks she had climbed with him. She still encouraged him to go to those places as long as he brought his visions and experiences back home to her. She lived for those things. And for every moment he was near her. But she could not be selfish, for even as a young girl, she knew he was a child of nature. A quiet and roaming soul born of wild places and drawn by whispering spirits that few can hear. This was the man she loved. The only one to whom she could have ever given her heart. In that, she was blessed.

With calloused fingers the man flattened a crease in the worn Indian blanket that was draped across her legs. "Becca," he began, "I want to build a fire at the edge of the yard tonight and make a place for us to sit and talk."

Becca questioned her husband with her expression. There was a hint of joy in his eyes as his chin tightened and his lips quivered.

Later that night as stars shone through the trees above them, he told her of his day and of the discovery he had made while walking by the music store in town. And when he finally unwrapped the treasure for his wife and brought his bow to its strings, her tears glistened in the firelight. For the tune her husband played brought with it visions of the sweetest and yet the saddest times in their lives.

The Heart of Virginia Festival is one of the largest one-day outdoor events of its kind in the state. Throngs of people migrate to Farmville each year on the first Saturday in May to experience the crafts, arts, and musical entertainment. No one in attendance is a stranger in town on that one day. And although the crowds can swell to over twenty thousand, the festival retains a hometown feel. It's a time when locals come out in the streets with friends and family and display their hospitality to outsiders.

The old man stood in the shade of a big maple tree and listened as Earl Carter, Jr., drove home the notes to "Rocky Top" on his banjo. The tall musician stepped up to the microphone and offered harmony to the final chorus of the song and then smiled as those in attendance clapped their hands. It was his final set of the day, and his shirt was wet with perspiration. Mid-morning until noon in the sun is a chore, even when one loves his task. Earl laid his banjo in its case and looked around for his wife and children. They were standing in line across High Street in front of the Lions Club hotdog tent. He closed the case and walked into the shade of the big maple tree.

"Good show, Earl." The old man in the straw hat

offered his hand, and Earl smiled and reached out to him.

"Thanks, Mr. Adams," he replied. "I believe I got a sunburn out here today."

The old man chuckled. "You fellas needed a tarp. Better put in your order for next year."

Earl smiled. "Well, I reckon we could have just moved right over here in the shade and no one would have minded." He looked at the hay bales roasting in the noonday sun. "Of course, the audience didn't fare much better."

The area was referred to as the Bicentennial Park. It was a grassy terrace with a center island of blooming flowers.

The old man pushed back his hat and wiped his forehead with a handkerchief. "It's warm for a May day. But at least it's not raining."

Earl agreed. He liked the old man. There was a sense of goodness in him. And he was a music lover, not just of bluegrass but of everything. It was evident in comments he made about other area musicians. He rarely missed a musical event in or around town. And Earl had heard the old man frequented recitals at Longwood and Hampden-Sydney Colleges. He liked all instruments, but preferred the sound of the fiddle.

"Are you going to play again, Earl?"

"No, that's it for us, Mr. Adams." He looked past the old man and waved at his wife and children. He shook the old man's hand and began to move toward his family. "You might want to listen to that girl standing under the oak tree, Mr. Adams." He pointed with a nod of his head as he spoke. "I don't know her, but I heard her playing for some children at a show we did last week. I couldn't believe what I heard."

The old man watched Earl join his family. Then he looked back toward the oak. The girl was gone. He scanned the area, but there were just too many people moving around. Besides, he had not even seen her face. He walked down the terrace steps and joined the mass of people moving along High Street. The smell of barbeque and cotton candy seemed a strange combination to him, but it caused him to pause on the sidewalk next to the Episcopal Church and open his brochure to the food vendor's page. He studied the choices but could not decide. Then the thought occurred to him that the sound of the crowd made him feel as he did at times beside a rushing stream. Alone and yet comfortable. He stood motionless and watched as the crowd passed by him. He thought it odd that at any moment, he could step into it and become a part of the movement, yet still be alone. He thought about Becca and how she had enjoyed the first few years of the annual festival. That is, until she could not endure the walking anymore. He missed his wife's company. He still went to places and events, but it was really not the same. Alone in a crowd, he thought. It must be a universal feeling. He listened to the passersby. He could watch their mouths move and hone in on a single voice. But it was faint. Just a snatch of a voice here and there, before they were as one. He looked up High Street at the craft booths. He turned and started in that direction, but then he stopped. There was music in the air. The notes came to him over the crowd noise as if they were bouncing upon the heads of the people. He looked for the source of the music, but he could not hone in on it. Not from where he stood. So he began walking through the crowd. The music began to fade, so he turned and walked back down the street, maneuvering through the crowd, toward the sound. He crossed the street and followed the notes as they beckoned him. When he stopped walking, he was standing on the sidewalk leading to Longwood College's Rotunda, where the artists and sculptors displayed their offerings. It was a little quieter here, and people with discerning expressions walked slower, hands locked behind them or arms crossed over their chests. His eyes took in the colors. And then, he saw a splash of color from behind a tree. That was where the music was coming from. He stood there and listened. Soon he saw the splash of color again. He walked slowly toward the tree, and when he was beside it, he looked in wonder at the source of the music. It was the girl from the oak tree across the street. She was barefoot and playing her heart out through an instrument tucked beneath her delicate jaw. As she played, her feet moved in the grass, and her long blonde hair blew in the wind. Her sundress flowed with her movements. She turned in circles and swayed her lithe body with the music. When the man looked upon her face, he saw that her eyes were closed. He knew the look. She was lost. Adrift in the music, as if in a trance. It captures a player, a good one who plays from the heart. One who lets go and allows his or her spirit to dance with the unknown. He had seen it before.

Within minutes a small crowd gathered around the girl. There were expressions of amazement and whispers behind cupped hands. A small boy stepped forward and approached the girl. She ended her tune and opened her eyes. And when she saw the boy, she reached out and took his offering with a kind smile. She tucked the stem of a flower behind her ear, then lifted the instrument, closed her eyes, and began to play a melody so touching, and yet unknown by all but one. When the girl finished her melody, she turned her head and looked into the tearful eyes of the old man. For a few moments, the sounds around her ceased, and she recognized something in the man's eyes that was familiar to her, and calming. She smiled timidly, then walked over to him. The little crowd which had gathered around the girl dispersed, melting into the passersby. A yellow-winged butterfly fluttered in the air between the girl and man, and the sound of its wing beats echoed in her mind. She could hear her own heartbeat before she spoke. "My name is Tillie O'Brien." Her voice was soft and clear. And in the old man's heart, it sparkled.

He smiled and nodded his head. A single tear began to course down his cheek, and he wiped it away with his hand. "And I'm Fate," he said. "Fate Adams."

"Come and sit, Mr. Adams." The girl moved toward a shaded marble bench a few steps away.

"Call me Fate," the man said as he followed the girl.

Tillie sat down next to her violin case. She opened it, retrieved a soft white cloth, and began wiping down her instrument.

Fate sat down just as a little girl approached.

"Will you play again for us, Tillie?" She looked back at her friends and giggled. "Please?" She was being coaxed.

Tillie looked at the little girl and then over at her friends. She smiled, nodded her head, and held up her index finger. It was a promise.

The little girl clasped her hands together and said in an excited voice, "Thank you, Tillie," and then ran to her friends.

"Your fans are unrelenting," Fate said as he watched the child rejoin her friends.

Tillie smiled. She placed her violin in its case.

Fate Adams leaned toward the girl and viewed her instrument. "May I?" He reached out his hands.

Tillie picked up the violin and gave it to the man. "It's not the best," she said as she let go of it. "But it's okay."

Fate examined the violin, turning it over in his hands. He plucked the strings with his thumbs. He held it at an angle and looked through the F holes.

"My parents said that one day they will buy a real nice violin for me." Tillie studied Fate's profile as she spoke. She was usually shy and not prone to carry on conversations, especially with people she did not know. But Fate Adams did not seem as a stranger to her.

"They didn't do bad with this instrument, Tillie," Fate said reassuringly. "It is a pretty good copy of a

Stradivarius. Somewhat common, but well-made. Perhaps turn of the century." Fate handed the violin back to the girl. "Do you know where they bought it?" he asked.

Tillie closed the case lid and placed it on the bench beside her. "They got it from Mr. Bailey," she answered. "He finds old violins and fixes them up."

Fate smiled. "Oh, yes. I know of Floyd Bailey, and I've seen your instrument before. I thought it was familiar."

"Really?" Tillie was impressed.

"Oh, yes. Floyd played that fiddle at a show a couple of years ago, and I saw it and heard it then. It's a nice instrument."

"Do you know anything about its history?" The girl was intrigued.

"Not much. Just that Floyd got the instrument from a fellow who said his father had acquired it from a luckless poker player. No one could play it, so it took up space in a closet for years. It was in pretty rough shape when Floyd got it. But he has a knack with old instruments and brought it up to snuff."

Tillie looked beyond the treetops. The sky was cloudless. A red-tailed hawk soared high above the festival. Tillie followed it with her eyes until it disappeared behind spring foliage.

"You know what I'd like to do someday, Fate?" The girl posed her question while searching beyond the treetops for a glimpse of the hawk.

"What is it you'd like to do, Tillie?" Fate looked at the girl as he questioned her.

For a minute, Tillie was silent. Then she looked at her new friend and confided. "I'd like to play my music around the world. I want it to soar like the hawk. I want it to touch other hearts the way it does mine. I want the sick to hear it and feel better. I want the dying to hear it and not be afraid. And I want enemies to hear it and forget their differences."

A boy called from across the yard. "Til, come and play for us." Children had begun to gather.

Tillie opened her violin case and picked up her instrument. She adjusted the bow strings and rosined them. Then she stood up and stepped out into the sunlight.

Fate Adams watched as a gentle breeze rippled the girl's dress. The yellow-winged butterfly appeared again and danced on the breeze between the girl and the old man. She pointed at it with the tip of her bow as it fluttered by on a graceful, yet erratic course.

"Do you think my dream will come true, Fate?"

Fate smiled and answered, "The question is, do you believe it, Tillie?"

Tillie saw the butterfly dart away above the crowd of people in the street. Then she turned to Fate, brought her violin into position and answered. "Any dream is possible when you can hear the flutter of butterfly wings." Her eyes sparkled as she turned and began to play for the children.

Fate sat, stunned at what he had just seen and heard. He wondered how he could tell Becca what he could hardly believe himself.

Floyd Bailey was about to sit down at the kitchen table with a steaming cup of coffee when the phone rang. He sat his cup down and stepped over to the kitchen counter where he turned down the volume on the radio. He had turned it up when WFLO's Henry Fulcher began his daily mix of country and bluegrass music. Floyd always smiled when the legendary radio announcer informed listeners that he'd be "bumpin' gums at 'em 'til three less than a dozen." Henry had just closed out a George Jones song and begun "Back Up and Push" by fiddle player Benny Martin when Floyd picked up the phone.

The call was from Mac Massie, who asked Floyd if he could play bass for a show at the Curdsville Community Center in Buckingham. The gig was Friday, and they would get together Wednesday to go over a few tunes. Floyd agreed. He thought a lot of Mac, a local singer and guitar player with whom he had performed over the years. They had played music together over WFLO's airwaves during the 1970s.

Floyd hung up the phone and turned the volume on the radio back up just as Henry announced the upcoming fiddle contest at Smalley's Strings and Things Music Store in Farmville. The event was in conjunction with the store's grand opening in July. Contestants would be allowed to perform one tune of choice. All ages were eligible. The prize would be a German-made Roth violin valued at approximately $10,000.

Floyd looked at the calendar. He sat down at the table and sipped his coffee. Then he reached to the middle of the table and pulled the diary to him. It lay atop a yellow legal pad on which were scribbled names, dates and a phone number.

"Barley and Mindy Fold." He whispered the names. "Deceased," he said aloud. Floyd underlined a name and phone number. There was only one Fold listed with a Lovingston address. John Fold. Floyd got up and walked over to the telephone. He switched off the radio and dialed the number. With nervous anticipation, he waited for the voice of one who could possibly tell him what he wanted to know.

After the fourth ring, someone answered, "Hello."

Floyd tried not to let his nerves show through his voice. "Hello. Is this John Fold?"

There was a brief pause before the man on the other end of the phone answered. "Yes, this is John Fold. Who's calling?"

"My name is Floyd Bailey. I live just outside of Farmville, and I believe I have something that belonged to your mother. Was her name Mindy?"

"Yes, sir. What do you have, Mr. Bailey?"

"I have a diary that was found in the bottom of an old trunk bought at an antique store several months ago in Tennessee."

"Mom's diary?" John Fold raised the tone of his voice.

"Yes. I believe it is," assured Floyd. "Listen. I'd like to get this back to you, and since I'm coming over to Lovingston this Saturday, how about we meet somewhere?"

"Are you familiar with Vito's on Route 29?"

Floyd could picture the little restaurant in his mind. He and Grace had eaten there several times over the years.

"I know it, Mr. Fold. What time?"

"10:00 a.m."

"That's fine. I'll be there."

"Good. I can't believe you have Mom's diary . We were just, uh, well, I'll tell you about it Saturday."

"Thanks, Mr. Fold."

"Thank you, Mr. Bailey. Goodbye."

Floyd hung up the phone just as his wife walked into the kitchen. "Who was that?" she asked as she poured a cup of coffee.

Floyd thumped the legal pad with his knuckles. "That was the son of the woman who kept this diary."

Grace sat down at the table and pulled the diary over to her. She flipped through the pages. "I don't know how you read this, Floyd," she said without looking up. She paused and studied an illustration of a lone gravestone in a little clearing surrounded by large trees.

Floyd sat down opposite his wife. "It wasn't easy, honey. Her penmanship is awful. But once you get the hang of it, you see that she wasn't a bad writer. There's a lifetime recorded in that diary."

"And, maybe, an answer to a mystery?" Grace raised her eyebrow as she looked at her husband.

"I'm onto it, honey," Floyd smiled. "I'm meeting with Mindy Fold's son, John, this Saturday at that little Italian restaurant we've eaten at near Lovingston. You know it. It's on Rt. 29."

Grace nodded her head. "Vito's."

Floyd continued. "I'll drop off that mandolin I fixed up for that fellow over in Shipman and then drive on over to Lovingston. It works out perfectly."

Grace Bailey saw the satisfaction on her husband's face. He was at it again, doing what he did best. Fixing things and solving problems. Give him a broken instrument and he'd fix it. Give him a mystery and he'd solve it. It was in his blood. And she knew that teardrop fiddle was on his mind. She had realized that when he first told her about it. He had to know about it. Where did it come from? Who had made such an instrument? Yes, Floyd Bailey was onto something. And he wouldn't stop until he found answers to his questions. Grace knew something else, too. She knew that no other instrument he had ever played affected him as had this one fiddle. It was an understandable obsession.

Tillie O'Brien washed the last dinner plate and handed it to her father. Eugene O'Brien dried it and placed it gently on the stack of plates in the cupboard.

"Thanks, Tillie," he said as he wiped off the sink rim with the dish towel. "Can you check and see if your mom is finished with her soup bowl?"

"Sure, Dad," the girl answered. She left the kitchen.

Her father slung the dish towel over his shoulder and leaned against the sink. He sipped warm tea from a blue mug and listened to his daughter's footsteps as she walked down the hallway. Eugene looked at the clock on the wall. It was eight o'clock. He turned and lowered his head to look through a cracked window pane into the back yard. The night before he had seen a doe and her fawns browsing at the edge of the yard. A green moth landed with a thud against the window pane. Eugene noticed the perfect markings on its wings. He reached out and clinked the window pane with his finger nail. The moth did not move. "Smart boy," the man said softly. "You are better off there than flying around with the bats."

The man finished his tea and rinsed out his mug. He laid the mug in the dish rack, then turned and walked out of the kitchen. He passed through the small, dimly lit den and down the hallway to the bedroom. He could hear his daughter's voice before he entered the room. He paused at the door and listened as she spoke.

"There were more people there today than I have ever seen before, Mom. I mean maybe thirty thousand! And I played the violin for a lot of kids. I played jigs and little pieces I made up. And you know that tune I've always played?"

"Yes, dear." Her mother's voice was weak but full of pride.

"Well, I played that one, and I saw an old man with tears in his eyes."

"Oh?" Mary O'Brien was interested.

"Yes, Mom," the girl continued. "He was just standing there. So I walked over and started talking to him." Tillie thought about the butterfly and how she had heard her own heartbeat. But she did not tell about these things. "I mean, it was like I knew that old man. He was so nice, and he knows about violins, too."

Eugene O'Brien stepped into the room. "Well, Tillie, did he tell you his name?" he asked as he sat on the edge of the bed and took his wife's hand.

"Yes, Dad. But it's a strange name."

Her parents looked at her and waited.

"His name is Fate. Fate Adams."

Eugene and Mary looked at each other in surprise.

"I've never heard of a person with a name like Fate," her father admitted. "Although Adams is a pretty common name. What did you talk about, honey?" Eugene was curious.

"Oh, he knows Mr. Bailey, who sold us my violin. And he told me that my violin is a good instrument that was made in Germany around the turn of the century. He said it's a copy of a Stradivarius. I told him that one day I am going to get a nicer one, but he said you didn't do bad with this one."

"I think I like Fate Adams." Mary patted her daughter's head as she spoke.

"Oh, Mom, he's such a nice man. I think you would

like him." Tillie looked at her father. "You, too, Dad." Tillie took her mother's soup bowl from the bedside table and walked out of the room.

Eugene looked down at his wife. "Do you think we should be concerned about this Fate Adams?"

Mary shook her head. "No, honey. Our daughter's a very good judge of character. If she says Mr. Adams is a good man, then I believe her."

Eugene knew his wife was right. He also knew he was over protective when it came to Tillie. She was their only child, and such an amazing talent. She had been called a prodigy by the age of five. And now at thirteen, she was sought after by orchestras, talent agents, and several prestigious music conservatories. Eugene wondered at times if his over protection was a hindrance to her progress as a musician. He had kept the agents at bay, and the music schools would have to wait. He wanted Tillie to have a normal childhood. Or as normal as possible. But he often found himself wondering what was normal for a girl who had taught herself how to read music. Tillie could play a complex composition after hearing it only once. And what was even more amazing was that she had written entire concertos by the age of eight. She loved Irish music and played reels and jigs and lullabies for fun and to entertain children.

Eugene and Mary O'Brien were so proud of their daughter, and yet they both shared regrets. Eugene's regret was that he was not financially able to give her the finest instrument, or even the best of anything. His salary as a security guard would not allow luxuries.

Mary's was the most troubling regret. It was not in her power to avoid or control the illness which had come upon her early in her marriage. Not often in her life with Eugene had she been able to hold a job for more than a year or so at a time because of her weakness. The multiple sclerosis had now disabled her to the point where she could seldom leave the house. She lived through her daughter and leaned on her husband.

As a young teenager, Tillie understood some of the concerns of her parents. And she made the best of every minute spent with her mother. She played her music every day and believed her mother when she told Tillie it eased her pain. She was a rock and the epitome of hope for her father, who was often quiet in his despair. Tillie O'Brien carried more upon her shoulders than a fair share of trials. And yet, she was happy, even thankful. For in her music, she found the perfection missing in her life. And one's ability to express her soul is a power unmatched.

John Fold stirred his coffee and watched the steam rise from his cup. He adjusted the window blinds so that he could look out at the parking lot in front of the restaurant.

"Can I get you anything else, John?" the young blond waitress asked.

"No thanks, Carly," John said as if he had been

pulled from a deep thought. He smiled at the attractive woman. "I'm just waitin' on some company."

Carly smiled back. "I'll check on you later, then." She walked back toward the kitchen.

A car pulled into the parking lot and came to a halt right in front of his window. John watched as a man who looked to be in his late sixties opened the car door and stepped out. The red-haired man stretched his back, then stooped and retrieved a brown paper bag from the car seat. He shut the car door and walked to the front of the restaurant.

Carly happened by the door as the man came in. "Good morning," she said in her most accommodating voice. Her blue eyes mirrored her pleasant nature. "Just have a seat wherever you like, and I'll be right with you."

"Thank you, young lady." The man smiled. "I'm here to meet John Fold. Can you tell me if he's here?"

Carly looked toward John, who was already halfway to the door.

"Here he is now," Carly nodded toward John, who reached out his hand and grasped Floyd Bailey's firm grip.

"Mr. Bailey?" John's voice was friendly.

"Yes," replied Floyd. "It's good to meet you. And just call me Floyd."

"All right, Floyd. Come on back to my table. I was just having a cup of coffee. Can I get the waitress to pour you a cup?"

Floyd followed John to his table and sat down. "Oh, no thanks. I drink a cup in the morning, and that's it for me. And I got an early start today. I had to see a fellow in Shipman about some business."

John nodded his head. He liked Floyd Bailey already.

Floyd had done a quick study on John Fold and, by the time he sat down across the table from the man, surmised him to be a family man, well known in the community, and a little nervous. The ring on John's finger, the fact that the waitress knew him by name, and the moist handshake told the former police investigator these things. He figured the son of Barley and Mindy Fold was in his mid-forties.

Floyd did not waste any time. He opened the brown bag and offered the thick diary to John.

"Gosh, Floyd." The younger man's eyes were wide. "I remember seeing my mama write in this book when I was just a boy." He examined the book and opened it to a middle page. Smiling, he commented, "She wasn't much for spelling, and her letters were hard to decipher, but she had a gift for expressing herself."

Floyd nodded his head. "She did that, John. She puts you right there. And there are some real good poems in there."

"You could make out her words?" John seemed surprised.

"Well, it took a while to get used to, but I got to where I could follow it pretty well." Floyd was actually proud of himself for his ability to read Mindy  Fold's handwriting and hoped that her son would not take offense to the fact that a stranger had read through his family's history. "I hope you don't mind that I read it, John," Floyd said as he folded the paper bag and set it under a glass ashtray. "I was given the diary by a person who found it in a trunk she had bought at an antiques store. The trunk had a false bottom in it, and the diary along with a fiddle were found in it."

"A fiddle." John did not seem too surprised. "Mama and Pop were what you'd call pack rats. They never threw away anything." John sighed. "A while after they passed, I auctioned off some things. I just didn't have room for it all. There were several old chests, and I thought I had gone through them pretty well." The man shook his head. "I wouldn't have imagined one of them had a false bottom." John was thinking out loud.

"Well, the folks sold the fiddle, but gave me the diary hoping that I could find its owner and get it back to where it belongs."

"How did you find me?" John sipped his coffee and settled back in his chair.

"That was easier than I thought it would be." Floyd joined his fingers on the table and rubbed his thumbs together while he spoke. "I called information and found there is only one 'Fold' in the telephone book for Lovingston." He pointed to the man sitting opposite him. "That's you."

John chuckled. "Well, I swear. Just to think this book was hidden by Mama in a trunk and then found and returned. I reckon I was supposed to end up with it." John leaned forward. "But you know, Floyd, she never said anything about it, and I think, maybe, it was because she was ashamed of being somewhat illiterate. You know, she always was real adamant about me learning and going as far as I could in school. She only went to school for two years. She came up hard, farming and all. And there weren't enough boys around to lend a hand."

Floyd understood. He had known plenty of folks in his lifetime who didn't have the education they wanted or the opportunity to get it.

"Your folks came up in hard times, John."

"Yeah, they did." John looked out the window. "They've been gone for almost twenty years."

Floyd nodded his head, but did not speak.

John continued. "Pop died first from the cancer, and Mama followed him a year later. They'd been together so long, you know. She always said she didn't want to stay here without him." John tapped his fingers on the table for a few seconds, then stopped. "She went to sleep one night and didn't wake up. I reckon that's the best way to go."

Floyd agreed. "I guess if we could have a choice, most of us would take that one."

John turned to the first page of the diary. He studied the writing and made out a few of the words. "Did you find anything interesting in here, Floyd?"

"Like I said, John, there's a lifetime in these pages. At least the lifetime with your father and you. You take your time with it, and you'll be able to read it."

Floyd had put off asking about the teardrop fiddle. But now he felt the time was right. "There is a family I'd like to know about, John."

"Who's that?"

"I want to know about the family who lived in Sassmo's Hollow. Your mama says in the diary that the place was left in your family's care."

John smiled. "That's right. It was, and still is. I watch over the place like they did. Nothin's changed there for over thirty years. We keep it up by painting, and we replaced the shingles a few years ago. But, really, it's still the same as I remember when I was a boy."

"Did you know the owners?" Floyd Bailey could feel his heart beating faster.

"Why, of course. Still do. I get a check from them every month for watching the place and keeping it up." John Fold had never talked about the arrangement made years ago, but he saw nothing wrong with sharing it with Floyd Bailey. He felt he could trust the man who returned his mother's most personal possession.

"Your mother wrote that the house belonged to a family by the name of Adams."

"That's right, Floyd. It belongs to Fate and Rebecca Adams. They live over in your neck of the woods, near Farmville."

"What can you tell me about them, John?"

"Why do you want to know about them?"

"Because Fate Adams paid a lot of money for the fiddle that was found in that trunk with your mother's diary. And I want to know why it's worth so much to him." Floyd had put it all on the table. He knew John Fold would either go the distance with him, or stop talking. He watched the younger man's facial expressions, his body language, and his experience told him a decision was being made.

"How much time do you have?" John finally asked.

"All day." Floyd did not hesitate in his response.

"Good, then." John stood up and dropped a few dollars on the table. He picked up his mother's diary. "You want to know about Fate Adams and that fiddle. So, I'm going to tell you. But I'm not going to tell you here. Come on."

Floyd pushed himself up from the table. "Where are we going, John?"

"Sassmo's Hollow," John said as he waved at Carly.

Floyd followed him out of the restaurant and started for his car.

"You better leave your car here, Floyd. We'll take my truck. It's a narrow and bumpy little road up the mountain."

Rebecca Adams moved slowly toward the front door. She glanced at the grandfather clock in the hallway as she passed by it. The time was 12:10 p.m. She had not heard the clock chime at noon. Perhaps she had dozed off in her chair by the den window. Then she remembered Fate talking about the fact that he seldom noticed the chimes of the clock at all. But let it become silent, and he was there to wind it within a minute.

At night when she lay awake beside her husband, she would count the chimes until Fate, somehow sensing her wakefulness, would bring her close to him. She would rest her head on his chest and listen to his heartbeat while he would remind her of a happy time they had spent together. Sometimes his story was of a walk in the woods on a crisp autumn morning, when a breeze had caused a rain of leaves to fall upon them. Or of a time on a cloudy day when the God light shone on a sparkling pond in a highland valley. And then, sometimes, he spoke of the things that caused her sleeplessness. Music that filled a little mountain hollow, and the daughter who had brought such joy to their hearts. Some nights, Rebecca would weep silently in the arms of her husband. But, always, she would find peace in his strength and assurance in knowing that she had been given the greatest gifts in life.

Rebecca stood at the screen door and watched her husband sitting in his rocking chair. The noonday sun crept up his pant legs, and she could see steam rising off his dew-laden shoes. No doubt he had been walking through grassy fields. But now he sat in silence, staring into the forest. A chipmunk darted across the walkway, but the man did not seem to notice.

"A penny for your thoughts, old man." Rebecca pushed open the screen door and stepped down onto the porch."

Fate was at her side in an instant, his strong hands supporting her as she steadied herself. He helped her to her chair beside his and settled her comfortably. Then he returned to his rocker.

"I was just thinking," he said as he reached down and brought the fiddle onto his lap.

Rebecca reached over with one hand and touched

the instrument. She closed her eyes for a moment and she imagined the face of a child. Then she looked at her husband and tried to smile.

Fate squeezed her hand. "Do you remember the last time she played for us, Becca?"

The woman nodded. "It was the most beautiful piece of music I had ever heard," she recalled. "Such a sad melody, with a chorus of such hope." Rebecca looked down at a flower print on her dress. "That is how I remember it."

Fate smiled. "Yes, of all the pieces she did, that one tune has never left my memory."

Rebecca listened as her husband spoke in a soft and trembling voice. "I hear it in my dreams, and sometimes when the wind moves through the pine trees. I hear it when rain blows against a window pane and trickles down like teardrops." Fate wiped his eyes and looked at his wife. He tightened his grip on her hand. "Becca," he started.

Rebecca studied the face of the man she had known since childhood. She waited for him to continue.

"Becca," he repeated.

"Yes, honey." She tilted her head slightly.

"I heard the tune yesterday at the festival."

"You mean you imagined you heard it."

Fate shook his head. "No. Well, maybe at first. But then I knew it was real. I mean it was like it was being played for me. I heard a jig being played, and I followed the sound across the street until I saw this young girl in a flowered sundress playing her violin in front of a group of children."

Rebecca was silent, her lips parted slightly.

"It was note-for-note, Becca." Fate assured his wife. "I couldn't believe it! But it seemed so natural for the girl. And when she finished the tune, she looked at me and smiled."

"Who is she?" Rebecca's voice was soft.

"She said her name is Tillie O'Brien."

"Was she playing with anyone else?"

"No, she was not a part of the festival entertainment. Just a young girl with a violin. She played reels and jigs and little pieces I've never heard before. It was her style that attracted me. It was so much like our Katie. So familiar. And then that tune, note for note."

"Tillie O'Brien." Rebecca said the name aloud. "Tillie O'Brien." She was remembering. "Oh, yes!" she suddenly exclaimed.

"What, Becca?" Fate sat up straight in his rocker and turned to his wife. "What?"

"It was a couple of years ago, in *The Farmville Herald*. An article about a local child prodigy." Rebecca Adams was proud of herself. She tapped the wooden arm of her chair with the palms of her hands. "Tillie O'Brien. The little girl who had never been given a lesson on a fiddle, but picked it up and started playing anything she heard. I remember now. Her parents couldn't explain it. They called in the heads of the music departments at Hampden-Sydney and Longwood to test her abilities to try to explain it."

"Well, did they?"

"No, the child would not communicate with

anyone except her parents. They had begun home schooling her because of some mental block she has about not speaking to anyone but them."

Fate recalled the day before when he had watched the girl play. Children spoke to her, but she had communicated only through her music. He had not heard her speak to anyone but him. "She spoke to me, Becca."

"You were over in Lovingston at the time, and I saved the paper for you. But I accidently threw it away." Rebecca shook her head. "I thought I had told you about her."

"No, I don't think I would have forgotten that."

"Well, the O'Briens live just up the road."

Fate was surprised. "Our road?"

"Yes. I know because Margaret Kachadorian told me so at the time. Margaret said the little girl's mother had been diagnosed with MS. I don't know what all has happened since."

The phone rang, and Fate arose from his chair and went into the house. Rebecca watched him leave. She reached over and picked up the fiddle her husband had left propped in his chair. It was still beautiful. She remembered how important it was to him to make an instrument for their daughter. Fate had made many fiddles in his life. He was known as "the fiddle maker" around the Lovingston area. And there were quite a number of musicians who owned his instruments. Most of the instruments carried a small wood-burned "Hand-Made by F. A." insignia on the inside. One could barely see it through the F holes. But the one he made for Katie held no such markings. Only mother-of-pearl teardrops inlaid into the front and each side of the scroll. And teardrops burned into the rim around the face of the instrument.

Rebecca Adams touched the teardrops with her fingers. She remembered her little girl. She recalled the music and the laughter. Those special moments for so few years. Three people, happiness, a family. Gifts to the heart and soul that could never be taken away, not even by death. Every day she remembered. It was a ritual. A tribute from her heart. Every day for over thirty years she set aside time to close her eyes and picture the face of her daughter. She could recall the warmth of a hug, or the feel of a small hand in hers. And then there was the music. The little songs they would sing together. The tunes that Fate had taught her to play on the fiddles he made. And then the ones she made up and played so proudly for her parents.

"Gifts from the birds and the butterflies," Katie had told them. "Just little gifts." Every day Rebecca closed her eyes and remembered. And every day, her heart broke. Then she would say a prayer and thank God for the little gifts that were not so small.

The old luthier could envision his violins in the wood he selected. He could imagine the music in an aged maple or spruce tree, or even the discarded boards and rafters from a renovated building. There was a beauty beneath the bark and the dark and dirty surfaces that only his eyes could see.

He bought the wood. He bartered for it. He salvaged it from anyone who could not recognize its potential. Then he brought it to his shop, where he cut, chiseled, and planed it into something beautiful and desirable. Something that could bring joy to one's heart. He worked with strong hands to assemble the pieces. The aged spruce top. The curly maple back and sides, carved and smoothed to perfection. His stained fingers joined the ebony finger board to the maple neck. He soaked maple ribs in hot water until they were pliable. Then he hardened them into shape in wooden forms he had made. He burnt a symbol into the wood from memory. He doubled the instrument's sides for strength, and fitted a dovetail joint. He cut and tapered a bass bar and placed it below the bass string. He added tuning pegs, a tailpiece and bridge. Then, with patience and skill, he masterfully placed a sound post through an F hole. With trained eyes, he examined his work. And when it was all done, he picked up the instrument and played the one tune that would test its worth and bring tears to his eyes.

"I don't know how you do it, Fate." Marty Hedrick examined the violins displayed along the wall of the shop. As usual, they were without question some of the most beautiful and well-made instruments on the market. Marty counted eighteen. "How can you consistently turn out so many violins in such a short time, Fate? It's amazing!"

Fate Adams sat on his stool and dusted his pants with his hands. A cloud of fine wood dust drifted to the floor and settled over long, thin wood shavings. The old fiddle maker stood up and reached for a broom. He dusted his shoes with it and laid the broom handle against the work bench.

Marty laughed. "Don't sweep the floor, Fate. I wouldn't think I was in the right place if the floor didn't crackle under my feet."

The old man smiled. He crossed the room and began carefully taking the new instruments off the wall. "Let's get these beauties packed up, Marty. If you are going to get back to New York this evening, you're going to have to hit the road." Fate lowered his head and peered over his eyeglasses at the young marketer. "I don't want you speeding back to the Big Apple. You have a little fortune on board, not to say anything about your own life. We've had a good thing going for a lot of years, and I'm too old to find another marketer here in the States." Fate wrapped the precious cargo with care, then he handed each one to Marty.

"Don't worry, Fate. I'm no fool. I'll be back home by eight o'clock tonight. I'll be on the phone with Phillipe after that, and we'll have those babies in Paris day after tomorrow. Phillipe has sold twelve of them sight-unseen." Marty patted Fate on the shoulder. "The European market for your fiddles has expanded to the point where I wish you would hire an apprentice, teach him your secrets, and mass-produce these beauties."

"Then they wouldn't be true Butterfly violins." Fate was serious. "Would they, Marty?"

Marty Hedrick understood Fate Adams. But he always had to make his hopeless suggestion. He knew the man would never give in. His violins were bringing top money from European musicians who had never been told their exquisite hand-made instruments were crafted by a luthier, who worked alone and might succumb to old age at any moment. They had no idea exactly who the craftsman was, for he had not signed or initialed his work for years. The only insignia on the instruments was that of a butterfly burned into the inside wood. One could barely see it through the F hole.

The European demand for the Butterfly Fiddles had grown over the past twenty years to the point where Marty Hedrick's trips to Farmville had become more frequent. He was dumbfounded that one man could turn out such a beautifully crafted instrument in little more than a week. But he had no idea of Fate Adam's work ethic, or any knowledge of what drove the man. He only knew that the Butterfly Fiddles were desirable instruments, and he was the marketer who had brought them to the attention of the Europeans. He also knew that if Fate would allow it, he could sell them worldwide. But Fate Adams would not allow it for reasons of his own. And Marty did not pressure him. He had resigned himself to the fact that Fate did not wish to be discovered. World-wide notoriety would be a hindrance to his quiet and unassuming nature.

Fate stood at the side door to his shop and directed Marty as the younger man backed his Suburban to the steps. A half hour later, he waved as Marty drove away, his SUV filled with boxes of Butterfly Fiddles. He looked into the trees at the green foliage that dressed the hardwood branches. A pileated woodpecker did its work on a hollow yellow poplar down the hill. The sound echoed through the forest. Fate breathed in the fresh mid-morning air and stepped back into his shop.

"Fate?" Rebecca stood at the door which led into the main house. Her husband lifted his eyebrows as he walked toward her. He put out his hands and led his wife into the shop. He pulled his handkerchief out of his back pocket and reached down and dusted off an armchair next to the wall. Rebecca sat down and settled into the soft, fat leather cushion. She straightened her thin, beige sweater as Fate pulled up a worn stool and sat opposite her.

"What, Becca?" he asked in a concerned voice. Seldom did his wife come into the shop, although it was connected to the back of the house by a glassed-in breezeway. She saw the shop as his place to think and work. Fate patted the back of her hand and waited for her answer.

"Mary O'Brien called while you were busy with Marty," she began.

Fate raised an eyebrow and turned his head slightly. "Mary O'Brien?"

"Yes. Tillie's mother."

Fate nodded his head almost as if he had expected it.

Rebecca continued. "She asked if her husband could bring Tillie over to see us. She said the girl has not stopped talking about you. And that she wants to see where we live, and to ask you something."

"Oh?"

"Yes. Mary is so excited that the child is opening up to someone besides them. She has that condition, you know."

"I know." Fate looked down at his shoe and picked a dried leaf off of his frayed shoelace. "Are you up to it, Becca?" he asked. "Are you ready to see and hear what I've told you about?"

The woman's eyes filled with tears as she swallowed and whispered. "I've already seen it, Fate."

Fate straightened and looked through the doorway that led into the main house. He rubbed his lips with his fingers and looked back at his wife's face.

"Where are they?" he asked.

Rebecca cleared her voice and answered softly. "They are in the den," she said while leaning toward her husband. "Eugene O'Brien is a nice young man. You will like him. And Tillie is...." Rebecca blinked her eyes and looked away for a moment before she could continue. "She's beautiful, and she spoke to me without hesitation. Her father can't believe it."

Fate touched his wife's cheek with the back of his fingers.

She reached out for his hand. "I understand now

what you felt." Rebecca spoke in broken whispers. Tears welled in her eyes.

"It's like a miracle." Fate wiped a tear from her cheek as he spoke.

Rebecca composed herself and smiled. "I can see it in her eyes. I hear it in her voice. I don't understand. But I know what I feel is true." She squeezed Fate's hand. "It's as true as my love for our daughter. And it's so deep within me that I want to hold this child in my arms. I want to thank God. But I'm afraid. What if it's just our imaginations? Are we just two old people longing again to see someone who was so special to us?"

Fate looked into the eyes of his wife. And there he saw the answer to her question. He smiled. "You know better than that, Becca. You see it in her eyes, just as I do." He paused for a moment and then asked, "Do you remember the butterflies?"

Rebecca put her hand to her mouth and thought back to a day so sad that she seldom went there. Tears spilled from her eyes as she nodded her head. She could not speak.

"Well," Fate chose his words carefully. "The day I met Tillie, she said that nothing is impossible when you can hear the wing beats of a butterfly." He knelt on one knee and embraced his wife. Rebecca cried softly on Fate's shoulder while he gently stroked the back of her neck and spoke into her ear. "All good things are possible, Becca. She belongs to someone else. But she is drawn to us. You can thank God for that without being afraid."

Rebecca breathed deeply and repeated. "All good things are possible."

Fate kissed his wife.

"Butterflies," she whispered the word.

"Butterflies," he said back.

Rebecca sat up as straight as she could. "We must always keep this to ourselves."

"Yes," Fate agreed. "She will deal with it her own way."

"We'll just be here for her for as long as we can be," Rebecca said aloud. "Like grandparents, maybe." Her voice was wishful.

Fate smiled. "I'm not going anywhere for a while."

Rebecca straightened her sweater and began to rise. "She's waiting for you, Fate. I'll get myself together and bring some tea and cookies."

Fate touched his wife's shoulder with one hand and her cheek with the other. "Are you going to be all right with this, Becca?"

Rebecca felt her husband's warmth and heard the caring in his voice. She pressed his hand to her cheek. "I will be."

Fate hugged her. He walked her through the breezeway and into the house.

Eugene O'Brien was nervous when he pulled his car into the Adams driveway.

"I knew it would look like this, Dad." Tillie

unbuckled her seatbelt and pulled herself up to the dashboard. She tilted her head to the side to look through the windshield at the roof of the two-story wood-frame house, which blended so well with the surrounding forest. "You'd never know something this nice was back here in the woods." Tillie spoke as she pushed open the car door.

"Wait a second, Tillie," her dad said, fearing she would be at the front door before he stepped out of the car. "Let's break the ice together."

Tillie waited impatiently while her dad got out of the car and walked around to her. Together they walked along a slate-and-gravel walkway to the front-porch steps. A welcoming voice came from the other side of a screen door. Tillie skipped up the steps and pulled on the door handle as Rebecca Adams pushed it.

The woman looked at the child and smiled. "You must be Tillie."

The girl did not speak at first. She stared at the woman intently for a moment.

"Tillie." Her dad put his hand on her shoulder and chuckled nervously. "Say 'hi' to Mrs. Adams."

The sound of her father's voice seemed to startle the girl from her daze. "Hi, Mrs. Adams," she said while studying the woman's face. "I met Fate at the Heart of Virginia Festival, and now, here I am." She stood there with bare feet, jeans, and a pink T-shirt.

"Well, it's so nice to meet you, Tillie," responded Rebecca. She extended her hand, and Eugene O'Brien grasped it and spoke. "I hope we're not coming over at a bad time, Mrs. Adams."

"Oh, no, not at all, Mr. O'Brien." Rebecca took a step back into the house. "Come in, please."

"Eugene." The man closed the screen door behind him. "Just call me Eugene."

Rebecca smiled. "Well, Eugene and Tillie, let's go into the den and visit for a few minutes." She led the man and the girl into a cozy room with an oval braided Indian rug and a brick fireplace. "Fate is busy in his shop, but he will be finished soon."

"Oh, a wood worker, or mechanic?" Eugene sat down on the couch and laid his ankle upon his knee. He fingered the stitching on his shoe with one hand, while resting his other hand on the cushion next to him. Tillie stood at the hearth studying framed photographs which crowded the mantle.

Rebecca took her seat next to the window. "I guess you could say he's a little of both."

Eugene smiled. "Multi-talented, then."

Rebecca agreed. "Oh, yes, that he is."

"Tillie told her mother and me that he knows violins."

The girl looked away from a black-and-white photograph of a child holding a fiddle. "He knows more than anyone I know."

Eugene and Rebecca waited for the girl to continue, but she did not.

"We bought Tillie's fiddle from Floyd Bailey a few years ago. He had bought it from someone and fixed it up. We couldn't afford to pay a lot for it, and he gave us a good deal." Eugene felt more relaxed now.

"It's hard to find good quality violins at reasonable

prices these days, Eugene. I hear Fate talking about it all the time." Rebecca got up and walked over to the hearth. "Fate says Floyd Bailey does good work and is fair when he sells an instrument."

"Oh, yes. Mr. Bailey knows what he is doing. Tillie has enjoyed her fiddle a lot. And she just seems to get better at it all the time."

Rebecca listened to the man speak as she approached Tillie. She saw the photograph the girl was looking at. "These pictures are of our family, Tillie." She pointed. "That's my mom and dad, and my brother. And over here is the only known photograph of Fate's parents." She pointed at another photograph. "I took this photograph of Fate trout fishing on the Piney River."

"And this is your daughter playing the fiddle?" Tillie knew the answer before the woman responded.

Rebecca smiled. "Yes. Her name was Katie."

"Was she a good player?" Tillie looked at Rebecca as she asked her question.

"Yes, she was."

"Tillie." Eugene stood up, his hands in his pockets. "You just met Mrs. Adams. Maybe she...."

Rebecca interrupted the man. "No, no, I don't mind." She looked back at the girl. "Fate taught her to play as soon as she could hold a fiddle and a bow. And by the time she was four, she could play anything she heard. She even made up her own tunes."

Tillie's eyes widened. "That's like me, Mrs. Adams! I can play. I don't know how I know how to do it, but I can play anything I hear. And I make up tunes all the time."

Rebecca could not take her eyes off the child as she listened.

"She's never had a teacher, Mrs. Adams." Eugene approached the woman. "When we saw and heard what she could do, we got some people to work with her, but nothing really came of it. Tillie taught herself to read music. And now she writes her own. A few years ago, I took some of her notebooks to a concert violinist who lives in Lynchburg, and she told me the pieces were the work of an advanced musician and composer. When I told her the notebooks belonged to my eight-year-old daughter, she was shocked. She couldn't believe it."

"Have you ever played with an orchestra, Tillie?" Rebecca asked.

"I did for a while," the girl answered, looking at her father.

"I work night security and couldn't get her to rehearsals," Eugene offered. "For a while, Mary was able to get her there and back, but with the MS, she doesn't have the strength to do it anymore."

"I play all the time anyway," Tillie chimed in. "I don't need an orchestra. I play for children, or for anyone who wants to hear me."

Rebecca knew that Tillie was trying to make her father feel better. She looked at her, standing barefoot in her house, so beautiful and talented. "Remember what you told Fate at the festival, Tillie?" she asked.

The girl pushed her long, blonde hair back over her shoulders with her hands. "I want to play my music for the world," she said with confidence.

Rebecca smiled. She knew about the girl's communication deficiency. She also knew that mental blocks could be dealt with. "Well then, if that is one of your goals in life, you must focus on it and overcome any obstacles in your way. An orchestra is a must. And there are special teachers who can help you."

Tillie looked at her father and then at the woman she had just met who spoke to her like a mother. She looked back at the photo of the little girl holding the fiddle. "Can I see Fate?" she asked quietly.

Rebecca looked at her and then at Eugene. She saw Marty Hedrick's Suburban come from around the back of the house. She touched the girl's shoulder. "Of course. Excuse me while I get him. I'll bring some tea and cookies."

"Please don't trouble yourself, Mrs. Adams," Eugene protested.

Rebecca was almost out of the den. "It's no trouble at all. You two just make yourselves comfortable. I'll be right back."

Tillie studied the photographs. She touched the one where Fate Adams knelt beside his daughter as she concentrated on fishing a dark pool with a long rod. "I love to fish," she said in a whisper.

"What, honey?" Her father stood looking out the window at robins feeding in the yard.

"Nothing, Dad."

76

When Fate entered the den, Eugene O'Brien turned and smiled.

Tillie walked directly over to the older man, reached into her back pocket and pulled out a rumpled piece of paper. "Hi, Fate." She spoke without hesitation.

Fate noticed the animation in her expression. There was a happiness in her voice. Her blue eyes sparkled with excitement.

"Hello, Tillie," he said with a smile. "It's good to see you again."

Eugene walked over and shook Fate's hand. "It's good to meet you, Mr. Adams." He squeezed his daughter's shoulder and looked down at her. "Tillie has spoken of nothing but you since she met you at the festival in Farmville."

Tillie looked up at her father and then handed the wrinkled piece of paper to Fate. "It's about a contest, Fate. And I want to enter it and win." She touched a small picture within the advertisement with her finger. "Look at the prize."

Fate smoothed the creases in the paper and quickly realized it was a flyer advertising a fiddle contest at Smalley's Strings and Things Music Store. Ben and Liz would open their music store on July 1st, and on July 3rd, a contest would be held where a person judged the best fiddler would win a Roth violin. Fate studied the violin as best he could. The flyer was one of many copies which he had already seen in and around town. It was not a very clear copy of the original flyer, and it was in black and white. "Um." Fate handed the flyer back to the girl. "That's the real thing there, Tillie."

He looked at the girl's father. "That's a nice instrument, Mr. O'Brien. German-made in the 20s." Fate pulled at his earlobe and squinted his eyes. "I can't imagine why the Smalleys would give away such a violin. It's probably worth over ten thousand dollars."

Eugene looked at the flyer his daughter held. "New-store publicity, I guess," he suggested.

"No doubt about that," Fate agreed. "Players will be coming from all around for a shot at that."

"But I'm going to win it," Tillie said confidently. Her eyes pierced Fate's. He was surprised at her boldness, but not her determination.

"What would she have to do to win it, Mr. Adams?" Eugene stood behind Tillie, his hands resting on her shoulders.

Fate did not look at Eugene. He studied the face of the girl for a moment. "You'd have to be the best, Tillie," he said in a serious tone. "You can't think you can win, or even hope that you will. You have to back up what you just told me. No room for doubt." The older man looked at the girl as if he were searching beyond her eyes. "Can you do that?"

"You've heard me play, Fate. What do you think?"

Fate folded his arms across his chest. He rubbed his chin with his thumb and glanced at Tillie's father, then back at the girl who was waiting for his answer. "The contest is in four weeks. You come back tomorrow afternoon and bring your fiddle."

Tillie smiled and looked at her father. "I can ride my bike, Dad, please?"

Eugene nodded his head.

Tillie's face lit up. "Can I come over at two?"

Fate offered his hand, first to Tillie and then to her father. "I'll be waiting."

"Tillie?" Rebecca called from the kitchen. "Can you help me with the tea and cookies?"

The girl rushed out of the room.

"Thank you, Mr. Adams," Eugene said softly. "I can't afford a new violin for her, and if you think she's got a good chance of winning, well, you know it's not like playing in front of children, or someplace where nobody expects anything." The younger man looked out the den window. "Have you ever heard a child play like she does?" he finally asked.

Fate walked over to the fireplace. He felt the smooth painted edges of the mantle with his fingers. And with his eyes he saw the smile of a little girl.

"What Tillie has is a gift." The old man turned and faced the younger man as he spoke. "Clinically and professionally, it's unexplainable. There are no experts who can tell you where her abilities come from. They use words like 'phenomenon' and 'prodigy.' But they stop short of saying what it truly is. A gift from God."

The sound of Rebecca and Tillie coming from the kitchen urged Fate to finish his answer so that no one except Eugene would hear him. "You ask me if I've ever heard a child play like your daughter? Well, I have. A long time ago."

"Thank you so much, Dr. Montgomery, that's great news."

Liz Smalley listened as her husband attempted to contain his excitement over the telephone. He looked at her and made the "okay" sign with his hand. "No, Dr. Montgomery. I think that if we open the hall by 2:30 that afternoon, we'll be fine. I'm not sure how large of an audience we can anticipate. But we have already heard from seventeen musicians. We hope there will be more."

Liz could feel her heart beat faster as her husband paused to listen.

"Thank you again, Dr. Montgomery. It's so kind of you to take care of this for us. We'll say a big 'thank you' to Longwood in the program. Yes. All right, then, goodbye."

Ben put down the phone and looked at his wife. His eyes were gleaming. "Wygal Hall is ours for the competition, Liz. Bruce Montgomery has arranged it. The doors will open at 2:30 p.m."

Liz walked over to her husband and hugged him. "Oh, honey," she said with relief. "I was worried we'd have to use the upstairs, where the acoustics are so bad." She looked at Ben and smiled. "The College really came through for us."

Ben squeezed his wife gently. "Yes. There is an event that morning and one the next evening, but our date and time are open. Dr. Montgomery even said he intends to come out for it."

There was a knock on the storefront door. "Just a minute," she called.

Floyd Bailey heard the woman's voice and turned the doorknob, pushing the door open enough to poke his head in. "Mornin' folks," he said as Liz reached to open the door.

"Good morning, Floyd." She pulled the door open and turned back to Ben. "It's Floyd."

Floyd stepped into the store. "I was just passing by and thought I'd see how things are going." He looked around with raised eyebrows. "You could open the store today," he chuckled. "The place looks great!"

"Oh, we're set here, Floyd," replied Ben.

Liz could not contain her excitement. "Tell Floyd about Longwood, Ben," she coaxed.

Ben followed her lead without hesitation. "Longwood has agreed to let us hold our competition in Wygal Hall. I just got off the phone with Bruce Montgomery." Ben was smiling.

Floyd was impressed. "Well, that's just great. Sound will carry much better there than it would upstairs."

Liz held up an unfinished flyer she had been working on. "That's all I need to put the finishing touches on this."

Floyd looked at the flyer. "Very nice, Liz. If you need me to hand out some of these around town, just holler." Floyd turned and put his hand on the doorknob. "I've got to move along now." He patted Ben on the side of his arm. "I'll check back with you soon."

"Floyd," Liz said his name almost as an after-thought. "Did you ever get anything out of that diary?"

Floyd opened the door wide and stood in the morning sunlight. "Well," he hesitated. "Yes. I was able to find out something about the woman who wrote it. She lived along Buck Creek near Lovingston, in Nelson County. I located her son and met with him and gave the diary back to him. He's a real nice fellow." Floyd wanted to leave now. He hoped the question of the fiddle would not come up, but he knew it would.

"How about that teardrop fiddle, Floyd?" Ben spoke with interest. "Did he say anything about it?"

Floyd did not want to lie to his friends. But there was an inclination not to go but so far when it came to the teardrop fiddle. In a moment's time, he searched for the right words. "Well, uh, Ben." He looked at Ben's face and then at Liz. "The guy knew his mom kept a diary, and he knew she had the fiddle. But he didn't know where either one was. He couldn't believe he had sold the very trunk that contained them. He had no idea about a false bottom in the trunk." Floyd hoped that was enough. He didn't feel right about going any further with it.

"Did he say that his mother played the fiddle?" Liz asked.

"He didn't say. But I don't think she did. She was just keeping it for an old friend," Floyd answered as honestly as he could.

Ben felt a rush of guilt. He shrugged his shoulders slightly before he spoke. "Golly, Floyd. I feel a little guilty for selling it. If indeed it belonged to someone else."

Liz had a look of concern on her face as her husband spoke. "I wonder if we did the right thing by selling the fiddle to that old man?" Her question was intended for either man.

Ben put his arm around the shoulder of his wife. "Maybe we could have gotten it back to whomever left it with her."

"Listen, you two." Floyd knew how far he wanted to go with his answer. And he decided how he could tell the truth without crossing the line he had drawn within himself. "There is a reason for everything that happens in this world, and maybe that fiddle ended up just where it is supposed to be." He nodded his head and turned to leave. "I'll see you soon," he said as he stepped out onto the sidewalk.

"So long, Floyd," Ben called.

Floyd heard the door close behind him. He sighed and walked along with the June sun on his face. Inside, he knew he had said the right thing.

Days later, Floyd stood looking out the window of Harry's Barber Shop on Main Street in Farmville. He watched as Fate Adams sat down on the bench across the street. Floyd had seen the old man sit there before. But he had never paused in his routine to talk with him. His brief conversations with Fate had always taken place during a break at a show, or sometimes before a local bluegrass show. Other than that, Fate Adams had always been just a face in the crowd. He had seen him sitting on the sidewalk bench as he drove through town. But he had never parked his car and approached the old man.

Floyd pulled his cap over his head. It felt a little loose after a haircut. He stepped out onto the sidewalk and gathered his courage. Courage he would not have had to garner, had he not investigated the man's life. Now Floyd knew a few things that set the old man apart from other men. Floyd crossed the street and approached Fate, who sat alone.

"Good morning, Floyd." Fate's voice was pleasant.

"Hello, Mr. Adams," Floyd responded.

"Fate," said the older man. "Just call me Fate."

Floyd smiled.

Fate patted the thin bench boards beside him with his hand. "Come and sit for a spell. The coolness of the morning is still with us."

"Thank you, Fate," he said as he sat down.

A cement truck turned the corner at Main and Third Streets and headed down Main Street in front of the two men.

Fate waited until the truck was at Dave Crute's store at the south end of the block before he spoke again. "I've been expecting a visit from you." Fate looked down at the sidewalk and then at Floyd. There was no hint of anger in his voice. He seemed calm. Floyd was not surprised at the old man's statement.

He knew that John Fold was in contact with Fate. Also, he had not asked the caretaker of Fate's place in Sassmo's Hollow to keep his visit there a secret.

"You've got a good man looking after your place, Fate."

Fate nodded his head. "Johnny's a good one. He comes from real good people. Mountain folk, plain and simple."

"Well, maybe not too simple." Floyd looked at Fate and smiled. "Mindy Fold was quite the writer, you know."

Fate agreed, "Yes. You know, it was only her lack of confidence that held her back from growing as a writer. Becca and I always thought she could have published something. You should have read some of her poems."

"I did."

"Well, then, you know she had good descriptive abilities. Heart and soul, too." Fate paused as if he were thinking back. "Yes, Mindy could have written a book, I guess."

"She just about did, Fate. I started reading her diary out of curiosity. I wanted to know who it belonged to. But then I continued reading it because I felt I came to know the people she wrote about."

"And what did you find out? " Fate looked into Floyd's eyes.

Floyd met Fate's gaze. "I found out where the diary belonged."

Fate nodded and looked across the street. When he spoke, his voice was softer. "And what about the fiddle?" Fate paused and then looked at Floyd. "What did you learn about the fiddle?"

Floyd Bailey's experiences as a state policeman and an investigator had made him a good judge of character. Instinctively, he knew Fate was a kind and gentle soul. Intuitively, he knew the man's heart was broken. Collectively, he knew that Fate Adams' pain and suffering were manifested through the fiddle that had miraculously come back into his possession. "I learned that some things are better left alone," he finally said. "I call what's in that fiddle magic. You know what really sets it apart."

Fate's smile could not mask the sorrow in his eyes. "Thank you, Floyd," he said softly.

A long minute of silence passed between the two men before Floyd spoke. "I found an old fiddle on the wall at Mottley's Emporium last week. It's in pretty bad shape, and I'm not sure if anything can be done with it." He hoped Fate would show some interest. He watched the old man's face light up.

"Bring it out to the house, and I'll take a look at it."

The two men shook hands as they stood to part.

"I'll see you soon, Fate." Floyd was glad inside that he had crossed the street, for the man he had approached out of curiosity had now become a friend.

Mary O'Brien pushed open the screen door with one hand as she leaned against the door frame. She held onto the door spring and stepped down onto a large, round piece of slate. She chose her steps carefully, her cane in her hand, as she made her way around the corner of the house. The late June breeze caressed her face as she rounded the corner to see her daughter sitting in a chair, quiet and alone. Sunlight shone through a maple-leaf canopy and dappled the blonde hair and shoulders of the girl. Her violin and bow lay across her knees. Butterflies fluttered about her, alighting on her shoulders and head. It was almost as if she wore a colorful crown of swallowtails, monarchs, and buckeyes. Mary watched in amazement as Tillie raised her hand and extended her forefinger. A pearly-eye butterfly rose rapidly from a nearby clump of grass and dashed at two others before winning a seat on the tip of her finger. Tillie giggled. She spoke softly to the butterfly, but Mary could not hear her words. A photograph could not have captured the beauty of that moment. But then, a photograph had not ever captured the profound beauty of Tillie O'Brien. How could it? She was a work in progress. Mary had known it since before the birth of her only child. She knew it when Tillie would move inside her womb to the music of Vivaldi and Mozart. She knew it when, as an infant, Tillie gazed into her eyes as "Conzonetta from Violin Concerto in D" played on the stereo next to her crib. And she knew it when, at the age of three, the child picked up a violin while visiting a neighbor and began playing the music she had heard all of her short life, note-for-note. Amazing was not really the word to describe Tillie. Phenomenal was hardly the term that could capture her musical ability. And yet, she was a well-kept secret in the sleepy little community in which she lived. Or perhaps one might say she was protected. Such is often the case for those who are labeled as "special." Tillie O'Brien wore the label well. And even she could not explain it. Tillie would hardly speak about it at all. And if she did, it was only to her parents. Experts could not expand their resumes or boast their success with her. But they did diagnose her at an early age with something they termed "rare." A social phobia, they called it. Selective mutism. It was beyond shyness and something that her mother had always hoped Tillie would outgrow. The experts agreed she should, someday. So Tillie stayed close to home, where she was loved, schooled, and accepted. When she reached out, it was through her music.

Rebecca and Fate Adams were the only people outside of Tillie's parents with whom she had ever spoken. She had been drawn to them, as a young child is drawn to his or her grandparents. Mary and Eugene did not understand it. But they were happy with it. In the weeks since the girl had met Fate and Rebecca, her mother finally could see a light at the end of a tunnel. The two older people had helped to boost Tillie's confidence in herself. It was Rebecca who suggested to the O'Briens that they rehearse small conversations with Tillie. That they role-play with her. And that they instill the fact that it would be fun to make new friends. It was also Rebecca who encouraged the girl to take part in small group activities. Tillie had begun to go to church with the Adams. And she had become involved with a youth group at the Methodist Church.

Tillie could hardly wait for Sunday, for the freedom it brought and the people she would meet. She was still very quiet, but now and then she would get a word or two out. And it felt good.

A shift in the breeze shuffled the maple leaves and daffodils, and the butterflies fluttered their wings and darted in all directions. One, a little brown-wing wood nymph, held tight to the end of Tillie's bow as she raised it and began to play. Mary had not heard the piece her daughter was playing. She listened for a minute, then walked around to a chair in front of the girl. Tillie caught the movement of her mother in the corner of her eye and continued to play until the woman sat down. "Mama," she said with a smile. "It's good to see you outside." Tillie held out the end of her bow so her mother could see the little butterfly. "He's stubborn," she said.

Mary reached out and tried to touch the wood nymph. It fluttered away. "Oh, well," the woman said. "Your fan only."

Tillie laid her violin down next to her chair. "I was thinking about the contest." She crossed her legs and folded her arms.

Mary was struck by her daughter's maturity. Tillie was thirteen and beginning to blossom physically, and there was something in her voice and her eye contact that told her mother she was no longer a little girl.

"How many pieces can you perform during the competition?" she asked.

"One." Tillie watched a silver-spotted skipper alight on her knee as she answered her mother. "Fate says he was told over twenty musicians are signed up. It's open, so some will come unannounced. Everything from mountain to classical music."

Mary wondered if her daughter was nervous. "I guess a lot of players want that Roth violin," she said.

Tillie squinted her eyes and threw her mother a sly grin. "Yes, but I'm going to win it," she said confidently.

"With that piece?" Mary was curious. "What will it take to win? Has Fate suggested anything?"

"No, not yet." Tillie swatted her hand at a gnat. "I've played everything for him, but he won't say which is best. He says that I will know what to play when the time comes."

"Are you worried, honey?"

Tillie flashed her blue eyes at her mother and smiled. "No, not really. It will come to me." Her voice was brave. But her mother knew her daughter well.

"There is a magic when you play, Tillie. It comes through your heart and soul. You'll choose the right piece, I know. When you play, just close your eyes and pretend you are playing to the butterflies."

Tillie listened to her mother. Then she got up and came over to the woman. She hugged her. "I will, Mama."

The girl picked up her violin and bow. "I'm going to ride over to play for Fate," she said. "Do you need me to help you into the house?"

Mary reached out and held the hand of her daughter. "No, honey. Your dad will be home soon. I'll just wait here for him."

Tillie reached down and kissed her mother on the forehead. "I'll be back in time to fix supper."

Mary smiled. "We'll fix supper together tonight. I feel pretty good today."

Tillie smiled and turned to leave. "Don't do anything before I get home. Promise?"

"I promise. Now, get going, and be careful."

Mary watched Tillie walk away. She stretched her arms and looked up into the maple tree. The drone of a summer day was peaceful. It felt good to be outside. The brown-wing wood nymph fluttered over her shoulder and settled on the armrest of Tillie's chair. Mary smiled. "She'll be back soon. Don't worry." She heard the front door slam and the sound of Tillie kicking the stand on her bike.

"Love you, Mama," the girl called as she rode off.

"Love you, too!"

A cloud passed overhead, and Mary watched shadows run from themselves across the length of the back yard. When she looked back at the armrest of Tillie's chair, the wood nymph was gone.

Floyd Bailey was careful not to jostle the upside-down pineapple cake Grace had prepared and wrapped up for the Adams. He closed the car door and walked carefully up the narrow slate-and-pebble pathway toward the front porch. Tucked under his left arm was the old fiddle he had bought at Mottley's Emporium in Farmville. The sound of a pileated woodpecker at work echoed through the woods. It was a sound Floyd had not heard for some time. He stopped and looked around. The Adams' modest wood-sided house was nestled among tall white oaks and maples. He was surprised to see hemlock trees, some quite tall, growing among the mature hardwoods. The landscape around the house was natural and devoid of grass. There were islands of colorful flowers, all mulched and well-maintained. He noticed a large, stone fire circle at the edge of the yard, where young hemlock branches shone in the morning sun. Floyd had enjoyed his drive along the narrow and winding woodland road which led to the house. At no time was there a break in the forest canopy over the driveway. It reminded him of another winding road he had seen in Nelson County weeks earlier. A hideaway, he thought. He should have expected that Fate and Rebecca Adams would find such a place as this. He had noticed the lay of the land as he drove in. The driveway meandered along the crest of a ridge which fanned out and sloped upwards. Deep hollows bordered the ridge and stretched out like the frame of a slingshot. Sparkling trickles of water could be seen deep in the hollows. The ridge road led into a wide, flattened area on which the Adams house was located.

The front door opened as Floyd stepped onto the porch.

"Good morning, Floyd." Fate stood in the doorway smiling. His white shirt was frayed at the collar, and the sleeves were rolled back to mid-arm. His faded blue corduroy pants were worn and thin. A beaded Indian belt brought color to his subdued apparel. His engineer's shoes were old and scuffed.

Floyd noticed fine sawdust on Fate's pant legs and a thin curl of wood stuck in the roll of one of his sleeves.

"Howdy, Fate." Floyd offered the cake his wife had wrapped in tin foil. "Here's a little something from Grace."

Fate took the cake as he stepped to the side to let Floyd in.

"She didn't have to do this, Floyd."

Floyd removed the fiddle from under his arm and held it down by his side. "Oh, listen. Grace is known for these cakes. She makes them all the time, and she wanted you and your wife to have one."

Rebecca appeared in the entrance hall.

"Becca," Fate urged his wife closer. "This is Floyd Bailey. I've told you about him. And his wife has sent us a cake."

Rebecca stepped forward and smiled. "Well, hello, Floyd. Fate has spoken of you over the years. It's good to finally meet you." She took the cake from Fate. "Oh, thank you. We'll have dessert for a week!"

Floyd chuckled. "It's real good, Rebecca. Might not last a week." He winked. "They usually don't at our house."

Rebecca laughed. "Come in the house." She started

toward the kitchen. "I'll put this away and get you a cup of coffee."

Floyd followed Fate into the den. "Oh, no thanks, Rebecca. I'm fine. I just wanted to see what your husband thinks of this fiddle."

"All right, then," Rebecca said as she disappeared down the hallway.

"Let me see that, Floyd." Fate reached out his hands, and Floyd handed him the fiddle. Fate walked over to the window and studied the instrument.

"Um." He looked up the finger board and ran his fingers over the joints. "Strong sides. Probably double linings." He felt the sturdiness of the fiddle. "Good dovetail." He noticed a missing tuning peg. "No problem with that," he said. Fate walked over to the corner of the den and picked up a bow. He spoke as he brought tension to the hairs. "It's a mountain-made fiddle, Floyd. Lord knows how old it is. Could they tell you anything about it?"

Floyd watched the older man tune the fiddle's three strings. He brought the bow up and drew the hairs across the strings of the instrument. "This fiddle was definitely made for mountain music. It probably had a brighter sound to it, but look here." Fate tapped the finish on the fiddle. "This is a thick, hard varnish. Gives it a hard sound. Not much tone. And it was applied badly."

Floyd could tell by looking that the varnish was uneven and thick.

"You'd do better to get that finish off, Floyd. And apply a thin one." Fate handed the fiddle back to its owner. "Give it a tuner peg and some new strings, and it should find the turkey in the straw pretty good." He smiled. "I love these old mountain-made fiddles. Can I ask what you paid for it?"

"Seventy-five dollars," Floyd answered. "I talked them down from one-twenty-five."

Fate nodded his head. "That's about right," he agreed. "Now, you fix it up and whether you hang it on a wall or play it on the porch, you'll have an instrument easily worth three hundred dollars."

Floyd winked. "That's about what I figured."

Rebecca walked back into the room. "Floyd, you'll have to bring your wife out to see us. I'd love to meet her." She walked across the room and settled down at the end of the couch.

Floyd noticed a basket which contained quilting pieces. Rebecca pulled the basket over to her and retrieved a long panel of cathedral-window quilting she had been working on.

"That's mighty pretty, Rebecca." Floyd watched as the woman held it up to the window.

"Thank you." Rebecca reached into the basket for her eyeglasses. "I like to make these cathedral-window quilts. And I had these Indian patterns lying around for the longest time."

"Oh, Grace will have to see that!" Floyd was impressed.

"She's done a store-full of those quilts over the years, Floyd." Fate was proud of his wife. "We've got them packed in cedar chests in three rooms." Fate saw a pair of scissors on the floor at his wife's feet. He walked over and picked them up and handed them to her. "We'll be back in the shop, Becca," he said softly.

The woman smiled. "All right." She looked past her husband. "You come back and bring your wife, Floyd. I don't get these brittle bones of mine out much anymore, and I would love the company."

"We'll do it, Rebecca. Grace would love to visit."

Floyd followed Fate out of the room. They walked down a hallway and into the kitchen, which was spacious and filled with modern appliances. A door led out onto a covered breezeway and into Fate's shop. When Floyd walked into the shop, he was instantly taken with its size. The room was approximately twenty-five by twenty-five feet. Its walls were covered with shelves and cabinets. Work tables were built along three sides. There was also a long, narrow work table in the center of the shop. Well-maintained electric saws aligned the work surface of one side of the long table.

Fate encouraged his friend to take his time and look all he wanted.

Floyd saw handmade tools. There were chisels and clamps, planes and rattail files. Drills and rasps and carving knives. Diagrams were framed under glass, which indicated how the tops and backs of Fate's violins were to be shaped, along with the areas to be dug out. A table had violin parts including maple necks, ebony fingerboards, spruce tops and curly-maple backs. Wooden forms held the damp maple ribs that would be the sides of the instruments. Carved wooden tuning pegs were arranged in a long, shallow tray. Lumber of various lengths and widths was stored carefully on one side of the shop. Floyd could tell that the lumber was not stacked, but placed in a way to insure proper aging.

When Floyd thought he had seen it all, Fate flipped a switch on the wall. Floyd's mouth fell open. Displayed on the wall, in a lighted glass enclosure, were ten of the most beautiful violins he had ever seen. Floyd walked closer to the display. He looked over at Fate, who stood next to the violins.

"Johnny told you that I am a fiddle maker."

Floyd stood in front of the violins and noticed their perfection. The scrolling of the necks. The slight deviations in color, from orange-brown to honey. Three of the violin tops were inlaid with a white-hickory strip.

"Yes, Fate. He said you are a fiddle maker." He spoke without taking his eyes off the instruments. "But there's more going on here than just fiddle-making."

Fate opened the glass door and took one of the violins off the wall. He handed it to Floyd. The younger man could feel its perfection. It's lightness. He had felt it only once before. "Are all of these teardrops, Fate?" he asked.

"No," admitted the older man. "There is only one teardrop fiddle."

Floyd turned the violin in his hands. He looked for a mark.

"Look inside the F hole." Fate helped turn the instrument so Floyd could see inside it. Floyd located a symbol and looked at Fate.

"It's a butterfly."

"Butterfly?" Floyd handed the violin back to its maker.

Fate carefully put it back on the wall and closed the case door. He walked over to a window and looked out into the woods. "I was a fiddle maker in Lovingston for many years," he began. "I learned from my uncle, William Henry Adams, and an old hermit fiddle maker, named Sassmo Campbell, who was half crazy and all gifted. The hollow we lived in was named for him. Sassmo took to us and left us the place when he died. Becca and I moved there soon after we were married. She made her quilts and baskets, and I made fiddles. It was just the two of us for a long time." Fate swallowed. He put his fingers on the window seat. "Things were good for us. I sold my fiddles mostly in Lynchburg and Charlottesville. And Becca sold her quilts and baskets on consignment at a shop in Lovingston. After we stopped thinking that we'd ever be parents, a little girl came into our lives. She was born when Becca was in her mid-forties." Fate took a deep breath. "Her name was Katie. She was the prettiest little blonde you ever saw. I guess most folks would say she was as wild as the woods she lived in. I mean, she loved the critters out there. She could make their sounds, and she could sing like a bird. She was always running to us with stories of what she'd seen or heard. But, if anyone would come around, she wouldn't talk. She'd wait in the woods until they'd leave. We thought it would be good to send her to school, but she'd have nothing to do with it. They couldn't get her to open up at all. So, Becca just taught her at home.

She wouldn't talk to anybody except us and the critters." Fate smiled. "But she would play the fiddle."

"She could play?" Floyd knew that Fate and Rebecca had lost a child. But he did not know what had happened. Mindy Fold had only gone so far with it in her journal, and her son would not elaborate on it after he took Floyd to her grave.

"I taught her to play when she was little. She'd always come around when I was working on my fiddles. So I showed her some things, and she took to it naturally. After a while you would hardly see her without a fiddle in her hand. She'd lie in the leaves and play to the treetops, making up her own tunes. She said she got them from the birds and the butterflies."

"You don't have to talk about this, Fate." Floyd's voice was gentle. "I came here as a friend, not an investigator."

Fate turned his head and looked over at Floyd. "I need to talk about her today, Floyd," he said. "It's been a long time, and I've been thinking about her a lot."

"I reckon coming across that fiddle in the Smalley's store was a shock." Floyd didn't really know what to say.

"Oh, I thought years ago that if we left the hollow and I didn't see that fiddle again, maybe the hurt would go away. So I left the fiddle with Mindy. She put it away. Never even told her son about it. I guess she thought I'd ask for it back someday."

"So the teardrop fiddle belonged to Katie?"

"I made it special for her. That fiddle was actually the turning point for me."

"Oh?"

"Yep. I made good instruments up 'til then, but it was the fact that I was making it for her that pushed me beyond what had become the norm for me. You see, she was special and needed a special instrument. One that could give her the songs of the birds and the spirit of the world she knew."

Fate looked at his friend. "You should have heard her play, Floyd. It was like nothing I'd ever heard. Becca and I didn't know what to do with her. But we knew that one day we'd have to make some decisions. Her talent had to be heard."

"What happened?"

Fate hung his head for a moment, then looked back out the window. "One day she told us she'd been having headaches. It must have been going on for some time. We gave her aspirin and planned on taking her to the doctor the next day. I was sitting on the porch with Becca and listening to a tune Katie was playing. We had never heard the piece before. And there she was just sitting in the yard, the sun was shining down on her long hair, and she was just playing like an angel. I asked her where that tune had come from, and she said the butterflies gave it to her. Then she lay there on the ground like I'd seen her do a thousand times before. And she played it again so beautifully." Fate stopped and closed his eyes. He could see his daughter in his mind. He could hear her play the tune he would never forget. "A gift for the world," he whispered, while moving his hand with the notes he imagined.

Floyd remained silent. He knew that Fate Adams had stepped out of time. He watched the old man and waited.

Finally Fate lowered his hand. He looked at Floyd with glistening eyes that told of sadness beyond words. "Butterflies," he said softly.

Floyd's smile was supportive, and in his eyes was the strength that Fate needed to continue on.

"I had never seen so many butterflies in one place. They came through the forest and down the hillside into the yard that day. And they fluttered above her while she played. It was as if they were dancing. When she finished playing her tune, she looked over at Becca and me and smiled. Then she turned her face toward the treetops and closed her eyes. The shadow of a cloud oozed up the hillside, like it was sneaking out of the hollow. And, one-by-one, those butterflies alighted on her forehead until they formed a crown. There was not one teardrop from her eyes, but there were a thousand and more from Becca's and mine when we held her in our arms. Some of our tears fell onto Katie's fiddle. The next day, I carved tears from mother-of-pearl and inlaid them into the scroll of the fiddle. I burnt teardrops into the hickory strips on the fiddle's top. Then, I wrapped it and put it away. I couldn't bear to see it." Fate pushed his hands down into his pockets. He turned toward his friend and sat down on a wooden stool. "You saw her grave?" he asked.

Floyd nodded his head. "Yes. The Folds have kept it up real nice."

Fate smiled. "After we laid her to rest, those butterflies covered her grave. It was a beautiful sight. And they still do it sometimes. Johnny tells me it looks like a flower garden. Becca says that each generation of butterflies is told the story of the little girl who filled the forest with music. What do you think, Floyd?"

Floyd's compassion was expressed through the gentleness of his expression. "I think Rebecca is right. And I think that some of the spirit of your little girl is still in that fiddle."

Fate stood up and walked over to a cabinet. He opened it and retrieved the teardrop fiddle, which was wrapped in the original soft burlap sack he had tied around it so many years before. He untied the string that held the sack snug and cradled the fiddle in his hands. "I feel her presence every time I pick it up. I should never have left it behind."

Floyd stood up and admired the wonderful instrument. "Well, it's back where it belongs now."

Fate laid the fiddle down on the table. "It's closer, Floyd," he said gently. "Just closer."

Tillie licked the chocolate from the tips of her fingers. "These are so good, Becca." She pulled a paper towel off the roll under the kitchen cabinet and wiped her mouth.

Rebecca smiled. "Put one aside for Fate, honey. He loves chocolate chip cookies right out of the oven." She looked at the door to the breezeway. "I'm surprised he's not in here right now. Wrap one and take it out to him, will you, dear?"

"Okay. I'd better get back there, anyhow." The girl wrapped a hot cookie in a paper towel and finished her milk in one last gulp. She picked up her violin case and headed for the back door. "See you later, Becca. Thanks for the cookies." She started through the door, then stopped and looked back at the woman. "Becca?"

"Yes, dear." Rebecca dried her hands with a dish towel and turned toward the girl. "What is it?"

Tillie smiled. "After I win that violin, I want you to teach me how to make one of those cathedral-window quilts. I was thinking one with musical notes would be nice."

Rebecca was elated. "Of course I will, Tillie. It'll be fun." She watched the girl leave the kitchen. Then she walked down the hallway to the den with a feeling that she could have skipped the distance.

"Fate?" Tillie called as she entered the shop. She walked across the room and set her violin case on the corner of the central work table. The back door of the shop was open. Tillie walked over to a window and looked out into the back yard. He was not there. She noticed a burlap sack lying on the corner of the workbench. She picked it up and looked out the window again. This time, she was able to make out the form of a man standing on the knoll in the woods.

When she stepped out the back door, she heard faint but familiar notes. She followed the music across the yard, where she entered a worn and narrow path which led through the hardwoods to the knoll. A black-and-blue-winged butterfly fluttered over her shoulder and darted along the pathway ahead of her. Tillie noticed other colorful wings fluttering among the lower tree branches. As she came closer to Fate, she saw that his back was turned to her. A ray of sunlight reached down through the forest canopy and touched the shoulders of the man she had come to know so well. A man who seemed as close to her as her own father. Tillie would never tell it to a soul, but on the day Fate Adams stepped out of a crowd and into her life, a void within her was filled. It was not a void from the lack of love, because her parents could not have loved their daughter more. And it was not a void left by the loss of a loved one. It was something else. Something beyond explanation for one so young. A flicker in the shadows of her mind. The hushed truth of a mystery. Tillie's pathway to the man who stood on the knoll in the woods was cleared before her birth. And it was as inevitable as the changing of the seasons.

A tufted-titmouse glided down from the branch of a nearby cedar tree and perched gracefully upon a thin limb of a young oak. Tillie saw the bird and paused beside a large maple. She leaned against the cool smooth bark of the tree and listened to the music of her heart. And when it ended, she wiped away a tear and walked to where Fate stood.

"That's the tune I'll play, Fate."

Fate looked calmly at the face of the girl standing beside him. He smiled as she reached up and touched the tear on his cheek with her fingers. "You knew I would play it, didn't you?" she asked as he handed her the teardrop fiddle.

The old man nodded his head. "I knew," he said.

A gentle breeze moved the treetops as Tillie took the fiddle from Fate and began to play. Butterflies fluttered their wings, and the birds that sang their summer songs became silent. A woman was drawn by the music along the pathway to the knoll, and soon, three hearts were joined again.

Later that evening, as Fate and Rebecca sat in their den, Fate cleared his throat and spoke. "I told Floyd about Katie, today." He closed his L. L. Bean fishing catalog and placed it on the table next to his chair.

Rebecca tightened the stitch in her quilt piece, removed her glasses, and looked at her husband. "Floyd is a good man. I could tell that when I met him this morning." Rebecca folded her quilt and set it aside. "There's wisdom in his eyes."

Fate rubbed his face with his hands and looked out the den window into a forest bathed in golden light. "The witching hour," he said.

Rebecca knew her husband's ways. If she did not pursue his initial comment, that would be the end of it. And the fact that he had spoken about their daughter to anyone was worth her effort to continue their conversation. "Did Floyd learn of Katie from Johnny Fold?"

Fate shifted his weight in his chair. "Johnny told him we had a daughter and showed him her grave. He said that Floyd wasn't pushy with questions, but he was real interested in the fact that I was a fiddle maker when we lived there. He wanted to find out as much as he could about Katie's fiddle. Of course, he didn't know it was made for her. Johnny doesn't even know that to this day."

"Floyd knows the story behind the fiddle now, doesn't he?"

"Yes. I told him. It'll be safe with him. I know it. You can tell when something will be kept between friends." Fate looked over at his wife. "I even told him about the butterfly fiddles I make."

Rebecca raised her eyebrows. Her husband had never told anyone about his business. He had been as successful as a luthier could hope to be, and yet, it was enough that his violins were sought after by foreign musicians. There had been times when she wanted to tell about his success, but it would have been against his nature to deal with the result of it. Fate was quiet and to himself for the most part. Fame would have only brought misery to a man with his simple nature. But she was glad he had told Floyd about the fiddles. And she was relieved that he had finally opened up to someone about Katie. It had been their silent sorrow for so long. She had dealt with it through her faith and involvement in church. Fate found his answers in trout streams and fiddle making. But together, they were strong, helping each other along the way.

"Did you tell Floyd everything, Fate?" Rebecca's voice seemed nervous. "I mean, does he know about Tillie?"

Fate shook his head. "No, Becca. How do you explain Tillie?"

A comfortable silence fell over the man and woman.

Fate had picked up the newspaper and started reading when the phone rang. Rebecca had gone into the kitchen to prepare supper. She picked up the receiver there. Thirty seconds later, she called to her husband as she hurried down the hallway. "Fate!" There was an urgency in her voice.

Fate met her at the entrance to the den. "What is it, Becca? What's wrong?" He could see the worry on his wife's face.

"That was Mary O'Brien." Rebecca took a deep breath and continued. "She says Tillie is not home yet."

Fate looked at his wristwatch. "She's been gone for more than an hour. Where's Eugene?"

"Mary said he's not home yet. I told Mary we'd go out and look for her."

Fate was halfway out the front door when he answered his wife. "Stay close to the phone, Becca. I'm going to drive out to the road and see if I can find her."

Rebecca's fear grew as she watched her husband speed down the driveway. Tillie had boasted that she could make the bicycle ride between the two houses in thirteen minutes. She should have been home an hour ago. The woman swallowed hard and walked into the den. She sat down at the end of the couch. The phone was an arm's length away.

Fate turned left onto the hard-surfaced road and drove at a slow speed toward the O'Brien's house. There was little daylight left, so he turned on his headlights. A reflection caught his attention immediately.

He accelerated his car. The reflection was approximately one hundred yards ahead. As he neared it, he noticed deep ruts and loose gravel on the shoulder of the road. He slowed his vehicle and finally came to a stop where Tillie's bike lay among scattered gravel and dirty grass. Fate turned on his emergency flashers and got out. "Tillie!" he called as he examined the overturned bicycle. There was no answer. He could see where the bicycle had slid off the road. He figured her front tire had hit the gravel and caused her to lose control of the bike. Just beyond the bicycle's front tire was a three-foot gully. An open case and a broken violin lay scattered along the side of the road. Fate looked over the bank and saw the girl lying motionless. "Tillie!" he called as he slid down the bank to her. She did not answer him. Fate got on his knees and hovered over the girl. "Tillie." His breathing was heavy. He put his hand on the side of her neck. "Calm down," he told himself. He looked at her form. She was not twisted, though he noticed a protrusion on her left forearm. There was a bloody scrape on her right cheek. He put his ear to her chest and listened for a heart beat. He thought he heard a moan. "Tillie, can you hear me?" He spoke directly into her face.

"Hey, down there, can I help you?" The voice was loud and unfamiliar.

Fate raised up on his knees and saw the silhouette of a man in front of his headlights. "Yes!" he answered. "Call the rescue squad and tell them a girl fell off her bike. She is unconscious, and I'm afraid to move her. Hurry, please!"

"You got it, Mister," called the man.

Fate heard his truck speed away. He examined Tillie's head as best he could with his fingers. There was moisture in her hair on the left side. Fate knew it was blood. "Oh, God!" His heart was racing. "Tillie. Hold on, honey! Help is on the way."

He rubbed her cheek with the back of his fingers. "I'm here with you, Tillie. I'm here." He felt her arms. She was cold. The buttons popped off his shirt as he ripped it off. He laid it over her arms and upper body.

Tillie moved.

"Can you hear me, Tillie? Wake up, honey."

"Tired," the girl said with a weak voice.

"I know you're tired, honey. But don't go to sleep. Stay with me." Fate held her hand as he spoke. "Help is on the way."

"I'm thirsty." Tillie's voice was almost a whisper.

"I know, Tillie. Open your eyes, honey. Can you open your eyes for me?" Tears began to flow from Fate's eyes. The helplessness he had known so long ago was coming back to him. He could feel it taking over like a dark shadow consuming him. "No!" he shouted as he raised his face to the sky. "No, God, no! Not again. I can't lose her again. I can't," he sobbed. "Please." Tears coursed down his face until, finally, he slumped and lowered his head over the girl. A vision of a child's face with sparkling blue eyes came into his mind. A single teardrop fell onto the lips of Tillie O'Brien.

"Katie." Fate's voice was steady but just above a whisper. He looked at the face of the girl and then up into the sky. Stars had begun to appear. "Don't leave me again," he pleaded. A star fell in the northern sky, and a gentle wind crept through the treetops.

"I won't leave you again, Papa." Her voice was weak. But her words were unmistakable. Fate Adams heard the voice and cried his heart out until help arrived.

The grand opening of Ben and Liz Smalley's music store was the talk of the town by the day of the much-publicized violin competition. Newspaper ads had been running in the *Farmville Herald* for three weeks prior to the date. And WFLO radio was blitzing its listeners with news of the store's opening and the upcoming event for ten days in advance. The Smalleys had decided to make the event a benefit for the local Habitat for Humanity, and spectators had come out to show their support. Liz could hardly believe that all but a dozen seats were occupied when the competition began that afternoon. An hour later, there was not a vacant seat in the hall. By that time, the fourth of five flights of musicians had finished their performances. Each flight was made up of six players. A single finalist would be chosen from each flight. And then, the final performances would begin.

Grace Bailey leaned over as the last violinist in the fourth flight walked to the center of the stage. She cleared her voice and touched Rebecca Adams' hand.

"Maybe he decided not to come, Rebecca. I mean, I wouldn't blame him. This is enough to get anyone's nerves in bundles."

Rebecca looked at Grace reassuringly. She squeezed her hand and said, "He's already here, Grace."

Grace turned in her seat with both hands on her armrests. She breathed a sigh, then relaxed in her seat.

Fate stood at the entrance to the hall. His form was almost a silhouette against the light in the foyer. Rebecca saw him step to the side as the door behind him closed. She knew he would come.

"You can do this," she had told him the night of Tillie's accident. She had waited with him outside the Intensive Care Unit at University of Virginia Medical Center for what seemed eternity.

"Can I?" he had asked her. Seldom in all their years together had Rebecca heard her husband second-guess himself. But that was an emotional night. A night when they had held each other for strength and courage. It had been a night when their fear of the present mingled with the painful memory of their past.

"Remember what Katie told us about her music, Fate?" Rebecca had looked into Fate's eyes and spoke bravely. "She said it was a gift from the birds and the butterflies."

"I remember," whispered Fate.

"That makes it a gift from God. And God gives gifts only to those who are willing to pass them on."

Fate realized the wisdom in his wife's words. "I'll do my best, Becca," he promised in a tearful whisper.

When the man in the frayed jacket and scuffed shoes took the stage that evening in Wygal Hall, only one in the audience could have realized his talent. Who would have guessed that an old man who carried his fiddle in a burlap sack could play with such conviction? Fate's choice of music was "Foxhunter's Reel," a traditional Irish tune. The audience thundered its approval. The judges were stunned and unanimous in their decision. Floyd Bailey could not mask his joy, and he smiled openly as his friend joined the finalists.

That evening the musical renderings were spellbinding. The audience could hardly contain its enthusiasm for the performances it witnessed. But there was only one piece that touched the inner spirit of everyone who heard it. And that was a gift from the birds and the butterflies played from the heart of an old man.

A bird sang its morning song from its perch on an upper branch of an apple tree outside Tillie O'Brien's bedroom window. Safe in her own bed, she recuperated from the skull fracture and broken arm she suffered from her accident days before. Tillie listened to the bird's song long before she opened her eyes. The warmth from the sun through her window felt good on her face, but she turned her head away from its brightness. She closed her eyes again. Memories passed through her mind, into windswept clouds. Faces appeared, and voices fell out of the clouds and descended into wooded hollows. They were clear for an instant, then distant but familiar. A painted lady butterfly left the petal of a sunflower and darted through a shallow forest, where it came to rest among a thousand colored wings upon a small mound in a stoned-in clearing. It was like a beautiful flower garden in the middle of a wood. A gentle wind brushed the wings of the butterflies, and a melody, soft and familiar, arose from their slightest movements. The taste of a teardrop and a beckoning voice awakened her inner spirit in a way her conscious mind could never fully understand. The voices of the four people she loved most in the world intermingled until she heard the words of only one.

"Tillie?" It was Fate Adams, sitting at her bedside. "Can you open your eyes?"

The girl felt the warmth of the man as he took her hand in his. "Becca's here with me, honey."

Rebecca bent down and touched the girl's cheek with her hand. It was cool and soft.

Tillie opened her eyes. "I heard your voices in a dream," she said. "I heard music, and I saw a beautiful flower garden in the woods. But they weren't flowers."

"Oh?" Eugene stood behind Mary, his arms around her waist. "What was it, Tillie?" he asked.

Tillie looked at her parents and then at Rebecca and Fate. "They were the wings of butterflies," she answered. "There were hundreds, maybe thousands of them."

Fate felt a hand on his shoulder. Rebecca swallowed and fought to hold back her tears, for she and Fate knew the whereabouts of the garden. And so did Floyd Bailey, who stood in the doorway of Tillie's room. Fate looked up at his wife and over at Floyd. He motioned for Floyd to come into the room.

"Look what Fate has for you, Tillie." Mary sat down at the foot of the bed as Floyd came into the room. "Hello, Tillie," Floyd said softly as he handed a violin case to Fate. "I'm glad to see you're doing better." He stepped behind Fate and stood next to Rebecca.

Fate opened the case and gave the Roth violin to Tillie. She held it with her right hand and gazed at it. "Oh, it's beautiful, Fate," she said. "But how did you get it?"

"He won the contest, Tillie," Mary answered.

Tillie looked at Fate. "You played the teardrop, didn't you?"

Fate nodded his head, but did not speak.

"And, you played our tune," she said knowingly.

"Yes," Fate answered.

Tillie's eyes welled with tears. She laid the violin across her chest and touched Fate's cheek with her hand. "Thank you, Fate," she said. Her voice was full of emotion. "I love you," she cried softly. "I love you all."

Fate smiled, his heart light with joy. "And we love you, Tillie," he said. He reached into the violin case and brought out the bow which he adjusted. Tillie handed him the Roth, and he began to play a melody so pure and sweet.

Floyd walked over to the doorway and reached down for the other gift Fate had brought for the girl. He walked back over and stood beside Rebecca. Mary and Eugene O'Brien saw what he held behind his back. He winked at them and waited for the tune to end. When Fate finished, he laid the Roth back in its case. He looked over his shoulder at his friend. Floyd unwrapped the teardrop fiddle and placed it in Fate's hands.

Tillie's eyes opened wide with excitement. "The teardrop!" she exclaimed. "What?"

Fate put up his fingers in a gesture of silence. "The teardrop fiddle was made for one who could hear the wing beats of the butterflies and realized her music was a gift." Fate looked at his wife and then at Mary and Eugene. He felt the strength of his friend's hand on his shoulder. "When you played it for the first time last week on the knoll behind our house, I knew it would never sound so beautiful in anyone else's hands. It belongs with you."

Tillie could not speak. She had stood behind the tree and listened as Fate had played the teardrop. And then when he had placed it in her hands and told her only to play from her heart, it was as if she had held it before. A delicate memory. An old friend. Its sound so sweet that butterflies had fluttered around her as she played.

Fate laid the fiddle by her side. "Remember what you said to me the first time you and I met?"

Tillie remembered. She touched the teardrops inlaid into the scroll of the fiddle.

"The gift is inside you, Tillie." Fate continued. "The teardrop fiddle is yours. Now, take it to the world."

Floyd felt a lump in his throat, but he did his best to smile it away. And although he would never fully understand the thread which had brought the people in that room together, he would also never deny that it was perhaps the greatest presence of love he had ever witnessed.

Epilogue

Twelve years passed. And in those years, Tillie O'Brien lost three of the four people who meant the most to her. On a late summer afternoon, a truck pulled into the front yard of a well-kept wood-frame house, nestled among the trees in Sassmo's Hollow.

Floyd Bailey had not been to the house since his good friends were laid to rest there. It had not changed. The tin roof was in good shape, and a fresh coat of paint had been applied to the siding. The yard was natural, with stoned-in islands of flowers and shrubs. Two high-back wooden rocking chairs on the front porch beckoned one to come and sit for a spell.

A young man emerged from the back of the house and approached the truck.

"That's Johnny's son, Rand," Floyd commented as he unfastened his seatbelt and opened his door. "He's been looking after the place with his dad since he was little." Floyd stepped out of his truck and extended his hand. "Hello, Rand. It's good to see you again."

"Yes sir, Mr. Bailey." The young man's voice was pleasant. "I've been expecting you." He watched as another man stepped out of the truck on the passenger's side, and then a young woman. He walked around the truck. "Mr. O'Brien and—Tillie?"

Eugene O'Brien shook the young man's hand. He was impressed with Rand's firm grip. Strong hands, he thought.

Tillie was just impressed, period.

"Hello, Rand," she said as she put out her hand.

"I hope you had a good ride up." Rand's eyes lingered on Tillie's face, although his comment was meant for all.

"It seemed a little less bumpy than I remember," Floyd answered.

"We get the tractor and blade on that road about once a year. And I guess you saw the gravel."

"Looks good," Eugene offered. "Much trouble in the winter?"

"Not too much." Rand closed the passenger door and walked around to the front of the truck with Eugene and Tillie. "But it's better to have a four-wheel drive up here."

For the next half hour, Rand Fold showed Tillie and Eugene around the property.

Floyd walked up on the front porch and sat in one of the rockers.

Soon Eugene joined him. "It's nice up here, and the house looks to be in good shape." He cupped his hands and looked through the front window. "Fully furnished, too," he added as he sat down. "I don't know, Floyd. What do you think of her coming here to live?"

"Fate and Rebecca left her the place, and with all the traveling she does with her music, she'll only be here a few months of the year. I think it's a musician's dream. Think of the music she can compose here."

"Yeah, but it's so secluded. Do you think she'll be safe?" Eugene looked up the wooded hill in front of them.

Floyd watched Rand and Tillie talking and laughing at the edge of the yard. "I think someone will make sure she's safe."

Eugene saw the two as they walked around the house. "What do you know about the Folds?"

"Fate and Rebecca thought an awful lot of them. Total trust there, as far as I could tell. And I know Rand's daddy, Johnny. He's a real good man."

"Know anything about Rand?" Eugene's concern was that of a father who realized his daughter wanted a place of her own. But he needed to ask all the right questions and get the answers that would give him peace of mind.

"I know he graduated from college a few years back and has helped his daddy with the family real estate business. But by trade, Rand is a fiddle maker."

"A fiddle maker?"

"Yep. And they say he's a good one, too. Fate would bring him to his house in Farmville and teach him." Floyd scratched his forehead. "Fate told me once that the boy had a natural gift for making fiddles. He let him use the shop around back."

"I saw it." Eugene seemed impressed. "That's a nice shop. And when Tillie saw it, she just about flipped. Fate must have told her about Rand somewhere along the line. But if she ever met him, she didn't say."

"Well, Eugene, with what Fate and Rebecca left that girl, she can live anywhere she wants to live. But if it's here, I think it's best to be happy for her. Some folks search a lifetime for a place like this and never find it."

Rand Fold remembered Tillie O'Brien. How could he forget the little girl who played the fiddle the way she did? The little girl who would hardly speak. He had seen her play once at an art festival when he visited Fate and Rebecca. But she would not talk to him then. That had changed.

"I've seen this before in a dream, Rand." Tillie stood beside the little cemetery lined in stone beneath the hemlocks.

"I was told you were out of the country when they died," Rand said as he pulled a weed from the foot stone of Fate Adams's grave.

Tillie was quiet for a moment. "They died three months apart. I said I'd see them as soon as I got back. I went on tour, and then...." Tillie noticed a yellow-winged monarch butterfly fluttering over the child's grave. It alighted on the grave, and was joined by others. "Look" she said.

Rand had seen the butterflies before. "Yeah. They begin coming in the spring. Sometimes they cover her grave. They come every day, until it turns cold. I've seen it happen since I was a little boy." Rand bent down and waved his hand over the grave. A few of the butterflies fluttered above the grave, but soon they settled there again. "I used to shoo them away when I was a kid. But five minutes later, they were back. I leave them alone now. You know, her name was Katie. My dad said she played the fiddle very well. She wouldn't talk much. She died of an aneurysm. Her death was hard for Fate and Rebecca. Dad says that's why they moved away. Can't blame them."

Tillie knelt down and placed a flower she had picked from the yard on the grave. Not one butterfly moved. A warm breeze crept out of the woods, and for a moment she imagined the little girl and the music she had known all her life.

"Let me show you the house, Tillie." Rand offered his hand, and Tillie let him pull her up. They walked to the front of the house.

"Is the door unlocked, Rand?" Tillie stood on the walkway, looking at the front door.

"Yes." Rand started toward the porch steps.

"Wait," Tillie called.

Rand turned around.

"Can I go in by myself for a little while?"

The young man smiled. "Of course you can, Tillie," he said in an understanding voice. "I'll be out back, in the shop."

"Making fiddles?"

"Always," Rand said as he walked away.

Floyd and Eugene had walked over to the little creek that flowed beyond the front yard. They watched as Tillie walked up onto the porch.

Eugene listened when Rand called back to his daughter. "Call me if you need me, Tillie."

"You know, Floyd. I think she'll be all right up here. I really do." Eugene sounded convinced.

Floyd could tell Tillie liked the place. And he was pretty sure he had seen a spark between her and Rand Fold. "I think you're right, Eugene," he agreed. "I think that girl is going to be just fine."

The sun fell behind the treetops, reaching its golden fingers through the hollow. A breath of air touched the knoll beneath the hemlocks, and butterflies fluttered into the front yard as Tillie O'Brien stepped through the door that Fate had opened.

Titles by Francis Eugene Wood

The Wooden Bell (A Christmas Story)
The Legend of Chadega and the Weeping Tree
Wind Dancer's Flute
The Crystal Rose
The Angel Carver
The Fodder Milo Stories
The Nipkins (Trilogy)
Snowflake (A Christmas Story)
The SnowPeople
Return to Winterville
Winterville Forever
Autumn's Reunion (A Story of Thanksgiving)
The Teardrop Fiddle
Two Tales and a Pipe Dream

The books are available through the author's website
at tipofthemoon.com or call (434) 392-5274.

Write to:
Tip-of-the-Moon Publishing Company
175 Crescent Road
Farmville, Virginia 23901

Francis Eugene Wood writes his stories from his home near Sheppards, Virginia, in Buckingham County. The award-winning author has been called "prolific" and "a natural storyteller." He is known for his rich descriptions of rural Virginia life and his unique ability to blend fact and fiction in a way that mirrors the world around him. His books are released through Tip-of-the-Moon Publishing Company, a company he owns and operates with his wife, Chris.